THE ABBOT
OF MONTSERRAT
OR
THE POOL OF BLOOD

A ROMANCE

WILLIAM CHILD GREEN

New Introduction by Frederick Shroyer

Volume II

ARNO PRESS

A New York Times Company
New York—1977

V. 2 c.1

Editorial Supervision: Leslie Ike

———◆———

Reprint Edition 1977 by Arno Press Inc.

Special Contents Copyright © 1977
  by Devendra P. Varma

GOTHIC NOVELS III
ISBN for complete set: 0-405-10135-X
See last pages of this volume for titles.

Publisher's Note: This book has been reprinted
  from the best available copy.

Manufactured in the United States of America

———◆———

Library of Congress Cataloging in Publication Data

Green, William Child.
    The Abbot of Montserrat: or, The pool of blood.

    (Gothic novels III)
    Reprint of the 1826 ed. printed for A. K. Newman,
London.
    Bibliography: p.
    I. Title. II. Series.
PZ3.G8274Ab5   [PR4728.G287]   823'.7   77-2038
ISBN 0-405-10137-6

THE ABBOT
OF MONTSERRAT

ABBOT OF MONTSERRAT.

A ROMANCE.

Printed by J. Darling, Leadenhall-street, London.

ABBOT OF MONTSERRAT;

OR,

THE POOL OF BLOOD.

𝔄 𝔯𝔬𝔪𝔞𝔫𝔠𝔢.

IN TWO VOLUMES.

BY

WILLIAM CHILD GREEN,

AUTHOR OF THE

FAYS OF LOCH LOMOND, SICILIAN BOY, THE PROPHECY OF DUNCANNON,
&c. &c.

A monk, I tell you—a resolved villain.   SHAKESPEARE.

VOL. II.

LONDON:

PRINTED FOR

A. K. NEWMAN AND CO. LEADENHALL-STREET.

1826.

The mounting terrors which strike young
Fernandez de Leon, son of a prosperous
but mysteriously missing farmer, and
his beloved,the wealthy Isabel de
Gracey are somehow tied to the evil
presence of the sinister Abbot Abando.

CHAPTER I.

Old Holyrood rang merrily,
That night, with wassail, feast, and glee.

SCOTT.

. . . .

I've but one friend, and him I'll share amongst you.

OTWAY.

THE passage was illumined, as already observed, by the feeble glare of a solitary lamp, and, as Obando speedily discovered conducted them to the secluded apartment (a small square room at the extremity of the avenue) appropriated solely to the use of Roldan, within which he was accustomed to pass the greater portion of his time, and which had long served him as a sleep-

ing chamber, and retiring room, whenever
he chose to be private, which had of late
been frequently the case; for the fortress
above, to which this cavern formed merely
a subterraneous entrance, although gene-
rally supposed to be the habitation of the
dreaded Roldan, and as such by historians
handed down to the notice of posterity,
was in reality at this period too old and too
much dilapidated to be a habitable abode
for any human being. Into this secure
little chamber, therefore, of which the walls
were earth, and the floor unpolished marble,
did the chieftain, without ceremony, usher
his new guest, as a place from which (owing to its peculiar construction) it was impossible, or at least highly improbable,
that a syllable of their secret intercourse
should be overheard. Obando entered
without hesitation, at the bidding of his
conductor, and suffered him instantly to
close the aperture which served as a door,
by sliding a huge wooden panel before it,
which it required all his strength to move,
                              and

and against which he then rolled an enormous stone, of a stupendous size and
weight, as an additional security. The
monk, as before observed, surveyed without emotion these preparations for their
privacy ; his mind was bent upon the dis-
closure he was about to make of his own
iniquitous intentions, and the probable reception his proposals might meet with,
from him to whose evidently impatient ear
they were speedily to be divulged.

The principal furniture of this subterraneous apartment consisted of a couple
of seats, placed there, it is probable, for the
accommodation of the chief and his lieutenant, the valorous Sebastian, to which may
be added a small stone table (perhaps some
relic of Moorish magnificence), elegantly
carved, whereon was still burning a massy
silver lamp.   At one end of this singular
bed-chamber (if so it might be called) was
kindled a blazing fire, probably the result
of Corvetta's affection for its lawless in-
mate, and the cause of her visit to the ca-

vern, as before mentioned; while on the other side was situated a couch, small in its dimensions, but adorned with exquisite furniture. Here then we must, for the present, leave the two brothers to their secret conference, the subject and issue of which will appear in due season. Suffice it now to observe respecting it, that, during its continuation, Roldan seemed often wrapped in intense musing, while Obando as often traversed the floor of the chamber, in evident anxiety for the event.

More than an hour was suffered to elapse ere any one of the banditti ventured to intrude upon their privacy. At length Sebastian, whose office it was in particular to communicate every trivial piece of intelligence to the ear of Roldan, approached with a heavy step, which occasioned a clank of his accoutrements, and gave sufficient warning of his coming, for the purpose of summoning his leader to partake of their festivity.

The principal apartment of the robbers, a rude

a rude and spacious cavern, formed by nature in the centre of a hollow acclivity,
was by this time handsomely enough illu-
minated with many a sable row of lighted
torches, ranged in regular order along the
sides of the excavated chamber. This
place was now appropriated, by the ruffians,
solely to the purposes of revelling, and
taking their meals; the principal whereof,
and that at which they all assembled, was
usually partaken of at about an hour before sunrise; albeit the preparations for it
had, on this occasion, been accelerated, on
account of its being the expressed wish of
Roldan that Obando should witness their
hilarity, and partake of their repast, ere his
return to the monastery, which he was
well aware must be before the hour of
morning vespers. Accordingly it was not
long before this singular banqueting-hall,
and the passages leading thereto, were fit-
ted up in a style of rugged magnificence,
which accorded admirably with the lives
and characters of those for whose conveni-

ence

ence it had been adorned.   In the centre
was placed a huge square table, part of the
spoil of some successful predatory excur-
sion among the farmers in the neighbourhood, which was covered with a coarse
black cloth, and on which were scattered
a variety of platters, flasks, and provisions,
as for the entertainment of a numerous
company; and a numerous company indeed was there assembled, to partake of
the coarse rustic dainties that were spread
before them.

Around this sombre table were seated,
in solemn silence, awaiting the arrival of
their chief, a band of the most remorseless
and ferocious-looking ruffians, that ever
were gathered together beneath the eye of
man.   The air of each was, at present,
both respectful and submissive, as the moment of carousal and intoxication had not
yet arrived.   Each however seemed anxious for the appearance of their leader
Roldan, and with it the commencement
of their tumultuous entertainment: yet
several

several minutes had now elapsed since the customary signal had been fired, which announced that the feast was ready, and summoned all to this nocturnal scene of revelry, and Roldan had not appeared; a circumstance the more singular, inasmuch as himself had just before desired them to hasten the repast; and it was in consequence of this delay that Sebastian had ventured to seek him in his chamber.

At length, in a thoughtful mood, accompanied by Obando and the lieutenant, Roldan slowly entered the festal cavern, from a passage which communicated with his own apartment, and was received by his associates with a loud and universal burst of welcome and applause. The roar continued for some minutes, and then again subsided into an obsequious silence. It was the first time they had seen their chief for three successive nights, during which period he had secluded himself entirely from their society, commanding them, after his usual mode on such occa-

B 4   sions,

sions, to remain immured within their
boundaries, nor attempt any enterprise of
risk, until himself should again be capable
of leading or directing the assault in person.   As soon as their unanimous shout
of greeting had subsided (which was in
reality heartfelt, for they were elated at
the idea of being shortly more actively engaged in their desperate function), their
eyes were involuntarily turned upon the
monk, who entered with him, and with
whom he seemed to have been holding
such important private conversation. Roldan, who had received their tokens of con-
gratulation with a steadfast mien, and an
unaltered brow, immediately perceiving
the suspicious curiosity his companion had
excited, coolly addressed them, ere he proceeded to his seat, in a haughty and elevated voice, to the following effect.—" I
bring you here, my gallant comrades," he
exclaimed, thrusting Obando forward to
their notice—" I bring you here a most
unheard-of prodigy—a monk in whom is

no

no hypocrisy—a priest without deception, who is our firm ally, and proffers to do us considerable service. Receive him into your community, of which he is hencefor-ward a trustworthy, though not an active member. He brings us news of enter-prise and spoil; let his welcome then be as unanimous as the booty will, I trust, be glorious, and your bravery eminent in the achievements of to-morrow."

As he finished, he took his seat proudly at what might be termed the upper end of the banquet-table, and motioned signifi-cantly for Obando to sit by his side. But the roof which had been rent with accla-mations bestowed upon the mighty Rol-dan, heard no shout raised in favour of Obando—the voices which had so willingly exerted themselves to salute their leader with a loud expression of delight, refused to hail the stern-looking monk with a cor-respondent sound of greeting. His very habit condemned him, despite even the praises of their captain, in the opinion of

B 5   his

his prejudiced beholders; they surveyed
him scrupulously, with a suspicious cold-
ness—wondered—grumbled in a whisper
to each other their disapproval of such
sanctified-looking allies, and again were
silent.

In a short time their jollity commenced.
Sebastian sat at the lower end of the table,
as second in authority; but attempted not
to check the riotous mirth, and boisterous
conviviality of his companions; for it was
a portion of their privileges, at that period,
to indulge in every kind of excess without restraint. Meanwhile the humbled
Corvetta waited diligently behind the
rugged seat of each coarsely-apparelled
ruffian, filling their cups with wine, and
performing other menial offices; for the
time had long gone by, although Corvetta
had not forgotten it, since seated proudly
by the side of Roldan, elated with the
pleasing consciousness of power and of
beauty, her very look had often controlled
the fiercest mood of the most sanguinary
amongst

amongst them; but the case was now different, and affected abhorrence (for tne
robbers, being sensible of her services, did
not in reality dislike Corvetta), or unmerited execration, were too often the only
rewards of her assiduity. Obando surveyed during the repast, with new and inde-
scribable sensations, the lawless band which
surrounded him; he remarked their brutal
conversation, contemplated their unfeeling visages, and shuddered at their viva-
city; but, in spite of the constant entreaties of Roldan, ate little, and spoke nothing.
At length, towards the conclusion of the
entertainment, as the wines (of which the
robbers seemed in possession of various
and delectable sorts, although their food
was but indifferent, and by far the worst
part of the fare produced on the present
occasion) began to take a peculiar effect
on the ' company, and 'increase their outrageous hilarity to a degree that was in-
sufferable, Roldan arose in silence, as if

disgusted

disgusted by the vociferous mirth of his associates, and motioned for Obando to follow him.

CHAP.

CHAPTER II.

Look, brither! look, the night's a' gane;
  The stars nae langer shine;
Sae now ye'll gae to yere ain gude bame,
  As I sall gne to mine.   *Scotch Ballad.*

THE monk Obando readily obeyed the
signal of Roldan to retire from a scene of
which (however its novelty might at first
have amused him) he was now in reality
weary; and as they quitted the cavern together, through an outlet different from
that by which they entered it, he heard
the chief whisper to Sebastian, who seemed to have wholly forgotten his superiority
of rank in the freedom with which he
mingled among his fellows—" See that
thy company be in readiness, by two hours
after noon, to perform a feat which will
put their boldness to the test: wait for me

an

an hour after sunrise, in my chamber, and I will there explain to thee the nature of this noontide enterprise. The division to which thou dost belong—the best of our whole troop—have I selected to perform this service. Promise them gold, Sebastian, the robbers' thirst and recompence; as much depends upon success, and a failure would be highly dangerous and disgraceful to our band."

Sebastian, bowing roughly, now retired to his associates, and the pair proceeded to the mouth of the cave. As soon as they found themselves upon the open heath, and beyond hearing of the banditti, who viewed with a scornful kind of pleasure the departure of Obando, the chief again addressed his companion.—"You see," said Roldan, " that we want nothing here but women to render our felicity complete; and one at least of that captivating sex thy scheme promises fair to bring amongst us. But look, Obando, the day is breaking yonder—it is time thou shouldst re-
seek

seek thy monastery. Let us descend; and mark, as we proceed, the course thou goest, that thou again mayst recognise it on thy return to our fastness, and so be enabled to scale the cliffs with safety."

The moon grew paler, and the voices of the banditti now gradually expired in the distance, as the monk (whom the appearance of daylight had warned of the necessity of his speedy return to the convent) and his conductor descended the steep and rugged eminence. The open tract in the vicinity of the cave was speedily cleared—the dilapidated fortress had disappeared also, or was but faintly visible—they passed the sentinel in silence, and entered together the craggy part of the mountains: anon they disappear in the deep bushy glens, presently they climb the elevated precipice, and now they sink again amid the thickening brushwood. At length they stood upon a little plain, nearly level with the convent, where they took an affectionate leave; Roldan having given

Obando

Obando the watchword, in order that he might pass the sentinel on the succeeding night, and repeating the word—" Remember !" as he again betook himself to the lofty abode of his companions.

The sun was just now peeping over the eastern promontories of the mountain, as the bell for morning vespers saluted suddenly the startled ears of the monk, and induced him to quicken his pace towards the private portal of the monastery.

Obando reached his convent just in time to prevent suspicion of his absence, by joining hastily the train of monks who were proceeding to vespers; and in less than five minutes he was kneeling with the rest, in outward semblance of holy worship, before the shrine of that all-seeing God whom his conduct had so justly offended.   At vespers were present, in addition to Ambrose and the brotherhood, the venerable Alfieri de Gracy, and his accomplished daughter Isabel, together with the youthful Fernandez, his intended
son-in-law,

son-in-law, and a numerous train of his
domestics. The soul of Obando became
fired with admiration as he gazed, from
beneath his dusky hood, askance upon the
glowing beauties of his intended victim,
and viewed with ecstacy those ripening
charms of which the yellow spirit had
promised him possession, and of which he
meant to deprive her ardent lover, in the
very moment of his triumph and fancied
security. The lovely Isabel was attended
as usual by the loquacious but faithful
Inez, whose principal grief on the present
occasion seemed a slight feeling of regret
that she was not so fortunate in the choice
of a lover as her mistress. In fact, the
imagination of this young lady, we should
not forget to mention, had been tortured
with nightly dreams and daily thoughts
of the obliging youth who had volunteer-
ed his services some little time back, so
gallantly in their cause; and conducted
them, amid darkness, peril, and tempest,
to the monastery. Carlossa had swam
hourly

hourly in her mind since their parting, and it was in vain she strove to banish his image from her recollection : she might never see him more—but the cast of his features, and his obliging conduct, to which even his ludicrous apprehensions gave additional weight and interest, she felt convinced were fixed upon her memory for ever : and if this was not the cause of the present slight shade of dejection which overspread her features, the writer of these annals, not being able to conjecture any other, must leave the origin thereof to his indulgent reader's penetration and sagacity.

CHAP.

CHAPTER III.

But his gaunt frame was worn with toil,
His cheek was sunk, alas! the while—
And when he struggled at a smile,
   His eye looked haggard wild.
Poor wretch! the mother that him bare,
If she had been in presence there,
In his wan face, and sun-burned hair,
   She had not known her child   Scott.

AND now the sun had arrived at his meridian height, and a throng of Alfieri's vassals and dependents were gathered around the portals of the monastery, who were clamouring as loudly as they dared at the non-appearance of their master; as this was the hour appointed for his departure to Barcelona, whence several of them had arrived that morning, for the purpose of escorting him home. In the hall stood the abbot, encircled by many of the brotherhood.

therhood, amongst whom Jacopo and the
malecontent were conspicuous; the former
awaiting with avidity an opportunity of
thanking the senors for the largess they
had bestowed upon the institution, in the
hope of rendering himself also the particular object of their charitable propensities; and the latter (Obando) lurking at a
little distance, as if to catch a parting
glance of her whose difficulties he was
well aware were not so nearly surmounted
as she seemed to anticipate.

Ambrose too appeared anxious to honour with a personal interview at parting,
the guests who had so unprecedentedly displayed their munificence in support of the
fraternity: for liberal indeed had been the
donations of Alfieri de Gracy and Fernandez, and handsomely had they contri-
buted to line the coffers of Ambrose and
his delighted brethren.

After a delay of some time, Alfieri de
Gracy made his appearance, and was speedily followed by Fernandez, conducting by
the

the hand the beauteous Isabel: they were instantly met by the principal domestic of Alfieri, who hastily informed his master, in answer to his inquiring glance to that effect, that mules were in waiting at the foot of the precipice to convey him to his residence near Barcelona. On hearing this intelligence, Ambrose and the rest of the brotherhood who were present (with the exception only of Obando), advanced to take leave of the benevolent agriculturist, and his amiable companions.

While this was passing near the outward portal of the edifice, the eyes of the fair Isabel were wandering involuntarily around her, as if taking a last leave of Gothic arches, gloomy pillars, and all the *et cætera* of monastic solemnity, until they fell once more upon the pale, lank visage of the retiring Obando, who was slinking behind an adjacent column, as if with a determined intention of watching her departure from his unenviable abode, although he dreaded observation while so doing,

doing, and seemed, moreover, particularly
solicitous to avoid *her* scrutiny. The eyes
of Inez, who still seemed inseparable from
Isabel, following those of her mistress,
also encountered his forbidding aspect, at
the same moment. Oppressed by their
united gaze, Obando shrunk into concealment as fast as he was able; but as his
visage receded behind the marble column,
the haggard features became faintly dis-
torted into a smile, which circumstance
escaped not the notice of Isabel and Inez,
although neither knew how to interpret it.

Isabel, although she knew not wherefore, felt an involuntary sensation of awe
at this unwonted and singular occurrence,
and notwithstanding she strove to conquer
it, a settled aversion to the malecontent;
while Inez whispered softly in her ear—
" Well, if there was not another living
creature, bearing the shape of man, betwixt here and the holy Jerusalem—whence
father Geronimo says he came some years
since—I think I should not wish to look
again

again on yonder ill-favoured churl! he terrifies me: who ever saw a smile so full of meaning, and yet so ghastly?"

Ambrose had by this time repeated again and again his wishes for their welfare, and safe journey to Barcelona, in which he had been constantly reiterated by the whining Jacopo, in conjunction with a few other over-zealous and superlatively hypocritical brothers of the order. Alfieri de Gracy and Fernandez returned their compliments as well as they were able, and issuing from the already-extended portal, bade what they hoped would be an eternal farewell to the monastery of Montserrat, where they had experienced indeed some kindness, and more good fortune, but where also they had found much canting and hypocrisy to be the order of the day, with little of real piety, or other Christian attributes, to bias the mind of a reflective observer in favour of its inmates. And here it may not be amiss to state more particularly the understanding

standing upon which our two lovers, Fernandez and Isabel, were permitted to accompany and congratulate each other; which shall therefore with brevity be explained.

On account of the dying concessions and earnest entreaties made by Velasquez de Leon, the father of Fernandez (and afterwards reported to Alfieri by that affectionate youth), joined to a phalanx of other considerations, more than sufficient to overwhelm any previous resolution which an offended father might have formed, Alfieri de Gracy had consented, without reluctance, to the speedy union of his daughter with the wealthy son of his deceased enemy—only stipulating, to which condition, moreover, Fernandez found it impossible to object, that a decent time should be permitted to elapse ere the consummation of their nuptials, in order that due respect might thus be paid to the memory of Velasquez de Leon (whom Alfieri de Gracy now professed the sincerest sorrow

row for having driven to such an extremity as forced him to adopt the popular re-
medy for disappointment—seclusion from
the world), and that Alfieri himself might
be better able to judge of the strength of
their mutual affection. These prelimina-
ries being settled, to which either party
cheerfully acceded—much to the gratification of the benevolent and well-meaning
abbot Ambrose, in whose deliberative
mind they perhaps received their origin—
there remained nothing but that they
should return speedily, and in amity, to
Barcelona; and the present was, as Obando had been previously aware, the very
hour appointed for their setting out.

CHAPTER IV.

—————————For several virtues,
Have I liked several women ; never any
With so full soul but some defect in her
Did quarrel with the noblest grace she owed,
And put it to the foil : but thou—oh, thou !
So perfect, and so peerless, art created
Of every creature's best.   SHAKESPEARE.

ACCORDINGLY. Alfieri de Gracy and his
companions commenced their journey,
walking as far as the bottom of the cliff,
where the mules were stationed ; to which
place they were accompanied by two of
the brotherhood, one of whom was no other
than the officious and communicative Geronimo.   As soon as they were mounted,
the monks returned to the monastery, after bidding their guests farewell with
much humility, whom, from pure motives
of

of courtesy, it appeared, they had attended to their saddles. Fernandez, however, suffered not Geronimo to depart until he had taken an opportunity of slipping unperceived into the hand of the good old sacristan (as he was called, although the distinction, as already observed, was little more.than nominal) a piece of money of considerable value, which he had reserved for the express purpose of rewarding his civility.

The party now proceeded at a brisk rate towards the base of the mountain, where was situated the village of Montrosol, having thus taken a last leave of the hospitable brethren—for hospitable the fraternity of Montserrat most undoubtedly were, although, it is much to be feared, their hospitality proceeded chiefly from selfish, or ostentatious motives; however, the three days' largess, with other benefits, universally accorded to travellers of every description, have been already hinted at; this was doing much to be called chari-

table, and surely those who have adhered
to it deserve to have gained the appellation.

The cavalcade, amounting in all to
nearly twenty, was attended by three or
four stout muleteers, whose voices were of
considerable service in accelerating their
pace; the mules in Catalonia being accustomed to pay more obedience to the voice
than to the rein, or even to the often
furiously raised lash of the driver. Already the huge cross of sculls had faded
from their view, and in imagination they
beheld the rustic habitations of Montrosol
peeping from between the foliage which
enveloped them: the pool of blood was
on the right hand of their uneven course,
and on the left an irregular tract of country, magnificently desolate, and peculiarly
adapted for the ambuscade of an enemy.

On arriving at this pass, the muleteers,
as if timid from habit, and wary from experience, unanimously urged their slug-
gish beasts to additional speed, and far
outstripped the unsuspecting Alfieri, and
his

his train of attendants, a circumstance
which was far from surprising him, as he
knew well the natural timidity and in-
tolerable superstition of that class of
people; and one which, moreover, gave
Fernandez considerable pleasure, inasmuch
as it afforded him an opportunity (freed
from the shouts of the drivers) of riding
at leisure, and conversing unmolested with
his-beautiful companion; for Alfieri de
Gracy had heretofore ridden in the van,
and was followed by Fernandez and Isabel, side by side; while the attendants,
out of respect, or a willingness to enjoy
their own conversation, rode clustered together at some distance in the rear of the
procession.   And never did Fernandez
behold his adored Isabel look half so lovely
as on the present occasion. Caparisoned
in her riding attire, and mounted on a
beautiful brown mule, whose skin was of
the most delicate softness, and whose pace
was nimble, airy, and graceful (even despite the dangerous descent in which they
c 3   were

were engaged), she might have been
deemed by an indifferent observer the
fairest of human creation, and in the eyes
of her enthusiastic admirer appeared a
perfect deity: the waving plume which
adorned her habit nodded gracefully over
her captivating form, her lovely hair
streamed loosely in the wind, or floated in
careless ringlets over her neck and shoulders, while the smile that irradiated her
blooming countenance spoke the rapture
of her bosom.   Fernandez gazed upon
her, as they proceeded, with an excess of
tenderness that, while it nearly approxi-
mated to adoration, softened the remem-
brance of his late mournful encounter with
a desponding parent, and the melancholy
scene which followed it: his eyes beamed
with enthusiasm, his heart glowed with
affection, his bosom heaved and palpi-
tated at the thought of his approaching
happiness, and he shrunk from imparting
his sentiments to her whose feelings he
well knew were in unison with his own.

Meanwhile

Meanwhile, Alfieri de Gracy still rode forward, following the course of the runaway muleteers, whom he yet descried in the distance, and whose discordant shouts, as they urged to faster speed the surefooted animals on which they rode, still faintly reached his ears. Presently, however, to his no small alarm and mortification, he beheld them disappear suddenly, and shortly afterwards perceived them winding among the crags upon the left, as for the purpose of eluding observation, whereupon he instantly halted, and awaited the arrival of Fernandez, designing to acquaint him with the circumstance, and his own suspicions of their treachery.

Scarcely however had Alfieri de Gracy staid his mule, ere a shot, fired from the brushwood near him, whizzed close to his ear, and assured him that his worst fears were but too well grounded; while a voice, proceeding from the spot whence the smoke now issued, exclaimed in a loud, harsh tone—" I could have taken a surer

aim,

aim, De Gracy, had such been my desire: attempt not therefore to escape, and no harm is intended you."

Alfieri de Gracy paused in sudden astonishment: what course was he to adopt, or how escape the threatened peril? He looked anxiously back towards Fernandez, raising his hand to his forehead, as if to assist his deliberations—a confusion of ideas assailed him, and he was motionless.

CHAP.

CHAPTER V.

In fuller sight, more near and near,
The lately ambushed foes appear,
And, issuing from the grove, advance.   BYRON.

. . . .

Good masters, harm me not !   SHAKESPEARE.

FERNANDEZ and Isabel were not far distant, and hearing the report of the carbine, instantly rode up to the disconcerted Alfieri.   In a few minutes the domestics also were alarmed, and crowded around their master, vowing to defend to the last gasp, should such a display of their courage be found needful.   Soon then were these valorous assertions to be put to the test; for scarcely were they uttered, ere a company consisting of some fifty assailants, whom their weapons, visages, and accoutrements, assured them were banditti, became at

c 5   once

once imperfectly visible among the pre-
cipices to the left, and struck the whole
party with horror and dismay. It would
be impossible to describe the consternation which ensued, among the meaner in-
dividuals of the cavalcade especially; although that very admirable description, by
a noble bard, of Hassan and his retinue,
might serve to convey a tolerably just idea
of the confusion that prevailed; while

> " With steel unsheathed, and carbine bent,
> Some o'er their coursers' harness leant,
>   Half sheltered by the steed ;
> Some fly behind the nearest rock,
> And there await the coming shock,
>   Nor tamely stand to bleed
> Beneath the shafts of foes unseen,
> Who dare not quit their craggy screen."

But what is most remarkable, and certainly might be said to demonstrate the
superiority of a Mussulman's courage, if
not his sagacity, was that the greater part
of the retinue of Alfieri de Gracy (in spite
of their stout professions when danger was
only apprehended) took to their heels and
fled,

fled, leaving their master and his beloved child, together with the few who chose to remain stanch by his side, entirely to the mercy of those whom they knew to be merciless, or at least believed so.

In less than another minute, a robber, who appeared to have some command amongst the rest, rushed fearlessly into the terror-stricken circle, and presenting a pistol to the head of Alfieri de Gracy, while with the other hand he levelled a second at the breast of Fernandez, who " wist not what to do," the occasion was so sudden, exclaimed in a rough, authoritative, and determined manner—" Stand and deliver! by command of him whose name, if spoken near this mountain, would make your very mules champ without grist or bridle, while they shivered with dismay, and your own teeth to chatter, like the visitation of an ague*—You, se-

nor

* The actual speech of a Spanish highwayman to an English traveller, and a fair specimen of the bombastic threats commonly made use of by these worthies on similar occasions.

nor Alfieri; and you, whom we know also,"
addressing Fernandez, " your arms, and
then your purses !"

By the time Sebastian (for the speaker
was no other than the lieutenant himself)
had finished this characteristic salutation,
the little group was completely surrounded by the banditti, who pointed their carbines and pistols each upon his chosen antagonist, and appeared ready to fire, upon
the slightest intimation of their chief to
that effect; while others, with drawn cutlasses, paraded on every side within their
vision, for the purpose of intercepting any
straggler who might otherwise be fortunate enough to overcome, or escape from
his antagonist. Among those who were
occupied in the latter mode, the keen eye
of Fernandez presently discovered the
very men who had acted as muleteers a
few minutes before, and who had undertaken to guide the party in safety to Barcelona. This discovery incensed him beyond measure; but it was too late, and a
little

little reflection made him feel how useless it was now to repine at his own want of discernment.

Alfieri de Gracy, in the mean while, knew not how to proceed; to oppose the will of these desperate marauders would, he knew, be to little effect, on account of his own inferiority in point of numbers and discipline, the greater part of his attendants, as already narrated, having deserted' him on the appearance of an enemy so formidable; and an encounter moreover with these unthinking wretches would endanger the safety, and might probably cost him the life of his child, who stood trembling, and watching his countenance, in the midst of the circle. He turned his stern glance for a moment upon her varying features, and this latter consideration, more than any deficiency in point of valour, or skill to use the weapons of defence with which he was furnished, determined him if possible to obtain a parley, and submit to their desires, rather than

risk

risk the consequences of an unavailing resistance. Accordingly the wealthy agriculturist, endeavouring in some degree to
abate the sternness of his looks, addressed
Sebastian, whom he took to be their leader,
as follows.—" If our arms and purses will
content you," said he, in a conciliatory
tone, " there is the latter," flinging his
purse to the lieutenant, " whose contents
are at your service; and here," he continued, drawing his rapier, " is my weapon,
which, as I am an honourable man, shall
also be surrendered, as soon as I have received some pledge that thereupon my
party shall pass without further molestation.—Fernandez, throw thy purse to yonder rough-headed, and, by the mass, rough-
handed fellow," alluding to a ruffian who
had rudely seized the bridle of Isabel;
" and let us, if it be possible, get on our
journey quietly.   Dost thou hear my
bidding, foolish youth?—obey me!"

" It is empty!" cried Fernandez, whose
purse indeed father Geronimo, and the
rest

rest of the good brethren, had lightened of all it contained—" it is empty, on my honour! and even were it otherwise, I would not yield it to so scurvy a summoner!"

" The yielding should nought have availed thee if thou hadst!" now shouted the lieutenant, scornfully.—" Hold fast the rein, Pedro! hold fast the rein!—Thou hast more wit, after all, than seems to abide in thee, and enough to shame the tardiness of thy superiors.—Fair lady," continued he, advancing with a saucy air to the side of Isabel, " we must trouble you to dismount: the path we have to trace is not easily accessible, and your weight will be sufficient for Sebastian's shoulders, without an added burthen of mule's flesh, to make him sweat the faster. Will it please you to alight therefore without further ceremony, or must my gallant comrades shew their mettle, by decapitating these your pusillanimous protectors?"

The

The answer to this question was a blow from Fernandez, which felled the interrogator to the ground, and this became the signal for a general engagement.

CHAPTER VI.

But who is she whom Conrad's arms convey
From reeking pile and combat's wreck away?

BYRON.

THE rest of the banditti, perceiving this commencement of hostilities on the part of their prisoners, as they had already imagined the surrounded party, now reduced to the number of eight, by the cowardly flight of Alfieri's domestics, very few of whom had remained to share the destiny of their master, lost no time in avenging the cause of their stunned leader in this shameful enterprise, of which it now appeared plunder was not the only purpose. Several discharged their pistols, while the greater number rushing towards De Gracy and Fernandez, bound and beat them severely in the course of a few minutes, after

after disarming them with ease, on account of their superiority in number, and their singular dexterity, produced no doubt by habit and experience in feats of this nature.

With regard to the domestics, they were easily overpowered; two were wounded mortally in the first onset of the banditti, and the remainder speedily took to flight, in which disgraceful course they were not checked by the robbers; for it now appeared no part of their scheme to intercept the menials of the party, or in any way molest them, provided the principal personages, Alfieri de Gracy, and Fernandez, together with the two females, fell easily into their hands. These therefore, with the exception of the lovely Isabel, were speedily secured and bound, and the two former treated with the utmost ferocity, for the resistance they had dared to make. And now the ruffians who had last officiated in securing Inez advanced boldly towards her mistress, with similar intentions; when

just

just as they were about to put those intentions into execution, the interference
of a tall majestic figure, evidently bearing
high command amongst them, from the
deference with which he appeared to be
treated, and who had been for some minutes past steadfastly regarding the trembling and affrighted damsel, induced them
to retire.

This was the universally obeyed and
dreaded monarch of those dangerous terri-
tories—this was Roldan! whose very glance,
even in a moment of irritation like the present (for the banditti were highly incensed
at the indignity which had befallen their
lieutenant), was sufficient to quell the au-
dacity, and temper the barbarity, of his
most hardened followers. He had been
in ambush near the summit of a neigh-
bouring eminence, watching the progress
of the party from the monastery, and purposed to remain a quiet spectator of their
surprisal and capture by the banditti in-
trusted to the command of Sebastian, on
whose

whose bravery and humanity he thought
he could rely ; but perceiving him fall at
the commencement of the contest, and
fearing greatly for the safety of the females, whom it was a part of his design to
preserve uninjured, Roldan had abandoned his concealment just in time to rescue
the fair maiden from the hands of her rude
assailants, ere she sank trembling and exhausted at his feet.

For some time the astonished chieftain
(to whom perfection such as Isabel's was
a sight as new as it was transporting) gazed
upon her in speechless wonder and admiration ; and then repelling with a haughty
look the officiousness of his rough comrades, who again advanced to bind her, he
approached to glut yet nearer his enrap-
tured vision, with beauty such as he had
never before beheld, nor dreamed to be in
existence. His band retreated submis-
sively to a distance, some hurrying to the
aid of the poor lieutenant, while others
prepared for a precipitate retreat to their
fastness

fastness in case of any surprisal, as the chieftain stooped amazedly over the drooping object of these newly-awakened sensations; until at length the distracted Isabel, perceiving the terrible situation in which she was placed, and recollecting the taunts and heavy usage Alfieri de Gracy and Fernandez had already endured, which it wrung her very heart to witness, faintly exclaimed—" Oh! shield my father, spare Fernandez, and pity, pity poor unoffending Isabel, who never injured aught to which God had given existence!"

Involuntarily did Roldan, on hearing this simple appeal to his humanity, uttered in a voice which seemed in reality to his ravished senses,

" Like unto lovers ears the wild words sung
In garden bowers at twilight,"

command his brutal associates to desist from further violence towards their unhappy captives, and again rivet his voluptuous

tuous gaze upon the lovely pleader for the lives of those she loved.

Anon a clattering sound was faintly distinguished, proceeding from a distance, and accompanied by the shouts of muleteers, which frequently in those mountainous regions prove the first indication of the approach of travellers. In a moment the chief caught Isabel in his arms, and bearing her up the crags with astonishing agility, gave the signal as he proceeded for the rest to follow him. The horde obeyed with surprising speed and regularity, carrying with them in like manner the two defenceless cavaliers, together with the affrighted but vainly-struggling Inez, and abandoning the wounded domestics to their fate; while Sebastian, whom the exertions of his comrades had by this time sufficiently recovered from his stupor, but who still severely felt the degradation he had so unexpectedly received, crawled sulkily after them.

CHAP.

CHAPTER VII.

I am not mad—I would to Heaven I were;
For then tis like I should forget myself.
Oh, if I could, what grief should I forget!
I am not mad—too well, too well I feel
The different plague of each calamity.

SHAKESPEARE.

IN vain did the lovely daughter of Alfieri de Gracy (whom the rude motion and novelty of her present situation appeared perfectly to have recovered from her amazement) implore the robber chief to inform her of his purpose, and request to be made acquainted with the worst she had to apprehend.   The seemingly bewildered and yet resolute Roldan spoke not a word, in spite of her many earnest supplications for an explanation of such conduct, as he bore the almost broken-hearted Isabel to his isolated habitation; still followed

lowed in his upward course by the stoutest of his associates, carrying, or now rather dragging, along with them the bruis-
ed and bleeding forms of- her affectionate
father and affianced husband, whom, even
in this wretched and helpless condition,
she still deemed it a kind of safety to view,
bound and often dangling in the greatest peril over the edge of some projecting
precipice, at the distance of only a few
yards beneath her.

On arriving at the romantic fastness of
the banditti, by the same steep and dangerous course which Obando had trodden
on the night before, and which it seemed
was the only path by which this singular
abode could be approached, Alfieri de
Gracy and Fernandez were unbound, but
instantly conveyed to separate dungeons,
where they remained, as appeared to have
been preconcerted before their capture (as
the robbers acted in this instance without
any visible signal from their leader, or
audible command being given respecting
them),

them , immured in total darkness, and un-
certain what kind of destiny they were to
encounter.

For Isabel, moreover, a different sort of
apartment had it seemed been prepared,
superior in comfort to the gloomy vaults
allotted to her protectors, and in which
Inez was permitted to attend her. The
door however of this ill-furnished chamber,
and the aperture which served it for a win-
dow, were strongly barricaded with iron
bars, a circumstance which, added to the
mysterious silence of the chief, assured the
despairing Isabel and her weeping attendant that they were considered as prisoners,
whose safe detention was a matter of no
trivial importance, and considerably aug-
mented their apprehensions for the issue
of this most unexpected and unfortunate
adventure.

To this solitary chamber therefore, after
her separation from the helpless companions of her ascent to this fearful spot,
from which it seemed probable they never

might again descend, was conveyed the frantic and imploring damsel, there to be imprisoned, until the result of the terrific captor's deliberations should be further known respecting her. Here her muscular supporter, who had hitherto borne her in his arms with much apparent ease, and whom, by the yellow feather in his cap, she now recognised to be no other than the notorious Roldan himself, left her to the care of her attendant, preserving to the last an uniform and determined silence with regard to her future destiny; yet Isabel thought that when, having laid his burthen on a couch that stood in one corner of the apartment, he turned him to depart, there was an expression of mingled sorrow and pity on his countenance, as if he was unwilling to leave her. She could not be sure of this; the light was hardly strong enough, in that gloomy chamber, to enable her accurately to distinguish his features; but Inez confirmed her in the supposition, that as he closed the door, he turned

turned again towards her with eyes so expressive of the tenderest sympathy, as
convinced them both that the feelings
even of the bandit Roldan were not proof
against the piteous pleadings of beauty in
distress, and that his sensibility was not
unmoved by the tears and lamentations of
his fascinating captive, nor his heart wholly
unaffected by the power of her charms:
and in this conclusion they were not deceived.   The susceptibility of the habitu-
ally proud-minded Roldan had indeed been
unexpectedly awakened at the sight of his
beauteous, unoffending victim, who he
well knew the achievements of that day
had doomed to certain and inevitable destruction ; nor was it in his power to avert
the evil destiny which awaited, through
his means, the ill-fated possessor of those
charms which had at once amazed and interested him—amazed him beyond expression, and interested him more deeply than
perhaps, even to himself, he chose yet to
acknowledge.

Roldan

Roldan had seen beauty before, had even revelled in all the warmest transports its caresses can bestow, ere his patrimony was spent among the partisans of folly and extravagance, and himself reduced to the necessity of becoming the desperate leader of a desperate horde of freebooters, for the purpose of recruiting his ruined finances; but beauty united to innocence, so attrac-tive, so engaging, it had never been his lot to encounter; on the contrary, so oppo-site had been those of the sex (with the exception of Corvetta) who had attracted Roldan's early attention, that he hardly imagined such to be in existence. No wonder then if the lawless chieftain felt, in its fullest degree, the influence of that captivating softness to which he was com-paratively a stranger; but, as Shakespeare says, "Something too much of this," unless we could divulge, and had moreover leisure to dwell upon the particular nature of the sentiments with which the beauty of Isa-bel had inspired him; and this discussion therefore

therefore (inasmuch as Roldan hardly knew yet the nature of those sentiments himself) must form the subject of succeeding pages.

Accordingly, to return to Isabel—her excessive grief at the horrible consciousness of being in the power, and even in the very hold of that ruthless marauder, whose name she had been taught to dread and execrate from her infancy, joined to her anxiety for the fate of those from whom she had been thus inhumanly separated, first vented itself in unavailing sobs and lamentations, until the unwonted exertion of her corporeal faculties, seconded by her incessant mental agony, soon threw her into a state of insensibility. On her revival, which at length was effected through the kind assiduities of Inez, aided by an elderly female (Corvetta), whose very appearance Inez afterwards protested was enough to scare any modern maiden out of her senses, the tender-hearted Isabel became delirious, and in her desolation would

rave loudly of Fernandez, of Alfieri, and
her own hopeless situation. This lasted
during the two first days of her confine-
ment, within which space of time, as Isabel knew little of what had happened, but
little of the occurrences that took place
will be here recorded. Meanwhile, the
intermediate space (first two days alluded
to, which Inez informed her had comprised
the whole duration of her malady) appeared to Isabel to have been passed in a
horrid dream, of whose appalling images
she still retained a faint and imperfect, but
terrifying recollection.

With respect to this imagined vision
(for it was only imagined—its substance
being, as Inez afterwards informed her,
no fiction of the brain, but a terrible reality),
the principal features that floated in her
memory, were the pale, gaunt visage of
the monk Obando, whose haggard aspect
again wore a ghastly smile as he surveyed
her, expressive of the most libidinous desires. This hateful apparition was succeeded

ceeded by a phantom no less singular, nor
(in the pure imagination of the unconta-
minated, sensitive Isabel) much more
pleasing in its appearance, namely, a tall,
unprepossessing figure, bearing the resemblance of a now faded, but once beautiful
female, who seemed to have forgotten every
softer attribute of her sex, and, in their
stead, to have assumed the habits and mode
of conversation usually witnessed among
the most depraved of the other. In addition to these appalling and disgusting objects, might be mentioned a fierce-looking
statue (for he spoke not, nor seemed in any
degree moved by her distress), with long
dishevelled locks, and a warlike countenance, whose features, if they partook not
of the ghastly expression of Obando's, were
indicative of a sort of brutal apathy, which
rendered him equally an object of fear and
detestation. With these moreover were
incessantly mingled the form of the fell
bandit who bore her hither, with his expressive eyes, and yellow plume, who

D 4 seemed

seemed grimly to console her, while his refusal to acquaint her with the fate of Alfieri and Fernandez served bitterly to aug-
ment her agonies.

CHAP.

CHAPTER VIII.

————How cam'st thou hither,
Where no man ever comes, but that sad dog
That brings me food to make misfortune live ?

                                    SHAKESPEARE.

IT was long before Isabel could believe the events she had witnessed, during the period of her delirium, any thing but the mere visionary creations of a disordered mind; but when at length the repeated assurances of Inez succeeded in convincing her, that what she fancied a mere feverish and unimportant dream was a mournful reality—that the pallid monk Obando had indeed stood grinning in horrid self-complacency before her—that Corvetta had indeed been commanded to assist Inez in hastening her recovery—that a savage-looking bandit had really stood beside her

D 5   couch,

couch, while he delivered their food to
her attendant—and, finally, that Roldan
himself had several times been in her presence, and even with his own voice essayed to soften her affliction—her tears
flowed faster than Inez ever remembered
to have witnessed them fall before. It
now appeared plain that Obando, the
dreaded, hated Obando, was the principal
cause of all her sufferings: she remembered
his grim smile on the morning of her departure from the convent, previous to the
capture and rout of her party by the banditti, and shuddered as she remembered it:
she doubted not this hypocritical monk
was in league with the banditti, and had
engaged with them to accomplish her destruction, and the overthrow of her protectors, an enterprise in which they had
too well succeeded. But to what purpose
was she confined here?—with what design had Roldan, and even the forbidding
ecclesiastic, visited her? These were
questions she strove vainly to resolve, and
of

of which she was at length obliged to abandon the fruitless and unprofitable contemplation.

In this state of suspense and terror, rendered doubly wretched by their total ignorance of the doom which Alfieri de Gracy and Fernandez had to endure, they passed the remainder of the third day till sunset. Corvetta was not in their apartment, having left it on the speedy recovery of Isabel appearing probable, as if previously commanded so to do by her superiors. Obando only visited the chamber for a few minutes, about the hour of midnight; and Roidan, they both guessed, would not again disturb them with his presence until the succeeding day.

Isabel de Gracy was still in tears—the wailings of Inez too were loud and frequent; but no one regarded them—no one seemed to hear them: all was silence around them, and they rightly conjectured that the robbers (as to sleep throughout the day, and their awake at night-fall, was

D 6   customary

customary among persons of that hazardous profession) had not yet arisen from their repose.

Night now gradually began to overspread the mountain, and darkness speedily pervaded their apartment, which they were without the means of dissipating, and therefore necessitated to endure: but, as might have been expected, with the approach of " raven-feathered night"—that season of love and enjoyment, but also of apprehension and iniquity—their terrors increased. Isabel flung herself mournfully upon an elegant sofa, provided by some strange means for her accommodation, again to meditate on the probable issue of this unlucky, and, she feared, fatal catastrophe, of her ill-advised elopement; while Inez, whose slender portion of philosophy was still less conspicuous, clung distractedly around her. At length the latter sorrowfully exclaimed—" Alack! to think the poltroons should so basely have deserted us (meaning the vassals of Alfieri), and

and left us to the mercy of a tribe of plun-
derers, more savage and ill-looking than
themselves! Oh, what a term of tribu-
lation have I passed since I quitted Barcelona on this foolish errand! what a
jaunt of accumulated terrors and misfor-
tunes has it proved to both of us!—that
grim, starved monk too, who frightened
us so at the monastery—oh, luckless ex-
cursion!—oh, false defenders!—and oh,
foolish Inez!"

Here the speaker paused, and wept
audibly for several minutes; until finding
she was not likely to obtain an answer,
and as talking is always some relief to an
afflicted woman, she hesitatingly resumed
—" Think you," said she, in half-deter-
mined and trembling accents—" think
you that our poor guide, Carlossa, as I
think he called himself, would have thus
forsaken us, had we chanced to require his
assistance in a similar affair, on our approach to the monastery? I am pretty
sure he would not, although I know not
                                        what

what induces me to think so. It is true, he looked not over valiant, nor spoke like one whose courage was likely to lead him into danger; but what of that? do you recollect his willingness to precede on the road?—and then his subsequent determination to return alone, with, above all, his unprecedented benevolence to the brotherhood—but I hate the brotherhood now— Heigh ho!"

Their apartment was by this time enveloped in total darkness, save the faint glimmer emitted by a solitary streak of moonshine, which entered with difficulty through the grated lattice, and was insufficient to disclose even the extremities of the chamber, both thought they now distinguished the sound of footsteps approaching the door of their prison, they listened accordingly, and were not deceived. In a few moments the grating key was turned, the bolts withdrawn, and a man entered, bearing a silver lamp, and a small tray of provisions. His face was concealed

concealed by a huge slouched hat, somewhat indicative of his profession; but
which, however, seemed to sit but awk-
wardly above the retiring countenance it
shadowed. The intruder silently advanced
towards a table, and resting the provender
and the light thereon, seemed again about
to retire.

"Stop!" cried Isabel, starting suddenly
from her posture of astonishment and dejection; "I will not taste your food unless you inform me for what infernal purpose I am detained here!"

As she finished this interrogatory, she
advanced some paces towards him, with a
majestic step and determined countenance,
on which the robber (for such she of course
conjectured him to be) as he approached
the door, with emphasis delivered his la-
conic message.—" Isabel de Gracy," said
he, with a significant gesture, intended to
inform them that he was watched, " our
captain, the renowned Roldan, desires you
to

to refresh yourself fearlessly; and after midnight, expect a visitor."

" Wherefore comes he?" again demanded Isabel—" wherefore comes he hither, and with what intent?"

" Ask me not now," replied he who appeared to be their gaoler, softly; then elevating his voice, and still making, as he spoke, significant gestures, to intimate to her that he was overheard—" of the secret intentions of the invincible Roldan, his humblest dependent can know nothing."

During the latter part of this response, his actions were so expressive of the fear he entertained of being overheard by some of the banditti, who it appeared were watching him, that Inez and her mistress could not avoid observing and understanding them. They saw, moreover, by his awkwardness under the habit which he wore (or at least fancied they perceived as much), that he was new to the profession which it seemed he had adopted; and already began to entertain some secret hopes,
from

from his evidently disguised demeanour,
that he might eventually prove a friend;
and these conjectures of his amicable dis-
position towards them, the following inci-
dent tended to confirm.

Just as he was about to close the door of
their prison, the robber who had been, as
they rightly imagined, appointed to bring
them light and food, for the first time
raised from his brow the huge-brimmed
hat which had heretofore concealed his features, and to their utmost astonishment
discovered the dark lineaments of Carlossa,
their former guide to the convent, on
whose supposed integrity Inez had been
expatiating only a few minutes before!
The countenance of the poor muleteer
was well remembered, even by Isabel, and
instantly recognised by her no less amazed
attendant, whose heart, in spite of the
despicable garb he had now assumed (even
more wretched in her eyes than that in
which she had first beheld him), under-
went a considerable degree of palpitation,

as

as she met his keenly directed and ena-
moured gaze.

Carlossa, the honest, industrious Carlossa, thus strangely metamorphosed into
a lower associate of these unfeeling ruffians, cast another compassionating look
upon the wondering Isabel as he retired,
and an arch glance upon Inez, which
plainly expressed that he had much to say
at a fitter opportunity, although but little
now as with an assumed appearance of
harshness, which also sufficiently demonstrated that his superiors were at hand, he
hastily closed the door, and locked it on
the outside with an air of petulance and
malignity. From this circumstance it appeared evident that Carlossa was now
leagued with the banditti of Montserrat
(as the lawless adherents of Roldan were
entitled); but it also appeared evident
that he had only lately and reluctantly
been made a member of their community.
It was plain too that he had recognised
them, and that he intended hereafter to
do

do something for their benefit, as soon as opportunity, and the perfect recovery of Isabel, concurred to aid him in its execution.

Meanwhile his wretched prisoners, thus left once more to bemoan their mutual helplessness, began to conjecture the name of this mysterious visitor, whose intentions the muleteer had been commissioned to announce, and vainly essayed to guess the purpose of his midnight interview. While they were thus employed, the heavy clanking of iron implements, as the wearer paraded to and fro, communicated the fearful intelligence to their minds, that a sentinel had certainly been stationed at the door of their dungeon, as an additional security, a circumstance which considerably increased their apprehensions.

CHAP-

CHAPTER IX.

Oh God! can it be possible I have
To die so suddenly? so young to go
Under the obscure, cold, rotten, wormy ground!
To be nailed down into a narrow place;
To see no more sweet sunshine; hear no more
Blithe voice of living thing; muse not again
Upon familiar thoughts, sad, yet thus lost—
How fearful! to be nothing! or to be—
What?—Oh, where am I? let me not go mad!
Sweet Heaven, forgive weak thoughts!   SHELLEY.

IT now becomes necessary to revert, for a
short period, to the wretchedly accommo-
dated Alfieri de Gracy, and his more ju-
venile companion in adversity, antecedent
to devoting our pages more particularly
to the elucidation of Obando's mysterious
projects, and depraved, but frustrated intentions.

Unhappily for De Gracy and his unfortunate

tunate fellow-captive, they had been thrown heedlessly into separate dungeons, and were consequently deprived of the little consolation they might otherwise have derived from each other's converse; which, however unavailing such intercourse might have been, as far as regarded any plans of escape contrived between them, would certainly have cheered away in some degree the heavy and darksome hours. But this was not all: the unhappy prisoners were not only thus prevented from holding any communication, but also sternly refused the slightest intelligence of each other, and even rigidly interdicted from mentioning the female partners of their captivity at all; whose very names, and capture altogether, the robbers who brought them food affected at first to have entirely forgotten: and afterwards finding that Alfieri was still importunate to learn the fate of his beloved child, and Fernandez that of his beautiful, affianced bride, these ruffians (authorized by the
brutal

brutal Sebastian, who still felt keenly the
smart of the indignity he had received)
threatened the supplicating captives with
instant annihilation, if they repeated their
inquiries respecting her.   Such, it is sufficient to say, was the situation of Alfieri
de Gracy : of the condition of the roman-
tically-attached Fernandez, it is necessary
to record something more ere we abandon
him, to pursue a no less interesting portion
of our narrative.

It was on the morning of the third day
of his imprisonment (although Fernandez
knew it not, for with him, as with the in-
carcerated chief of the Ægean pirates—

> "——long—anxious—weary—still—the same
> Rolled day and night,"

his dungeon being perpetually in darkness), as the youth was stretched despond-
ingly upon the hard floor of his cell, la-
menting in deep groans his piteous destiny, that he heard the bolts slowly removed, and the key turn softly in the
                                                            massy

massy iron-plated door. The difficulty
which seemed to attend the turning of
the key, and the time occupied in drawing
aside the bolts, bespoke the hand which
essayed it but little practised in the removal of those ponderous bars of metal,
or the adroit wielding of that massive key.
At length, however, the door burst open,
and for the first time since the dawn of
his captivity, he beheld a woman enter,
clad in a loose tattered garb, which very
ill became the majesty of her gait and aspect; the former being truly noble, and
the latter expressive of a spirit depressed,
but not subdued, by her outward degradation. With a firm, cautious step she
advanced some paces towards him, leaving
the door just sufficiently open to admit a
ray of light into the dungeon, and appeared steadfastly to examine his person
and features, as he lay extended on the
ground before her. Fernandez encountered her scrutinizing glance with an eye
of suspicious inquiry, which, if not so
eager

eager in its expression, was at least full as penetrating as her own. For some time she gazed on him with a degree of perturbation of which Fernandez little knew the meaning (conceiving it to be excited by mere compassion for his deplorable state), and then, perceiving him about to speak, significantly exclaimed—"Hush!—peace!" she muttered, softly placing her hand involuntarily upon her heart, as if to bid that sympathy subside which Fernandez knew not how he had awakened, "the lamb should not bleat when the wolf is near at hand. Be silent, and observe; and yet," she continued, in a tender strain, "why, why should I check that once dear voice, whose long-forgotten tones I came hither to hear? Thou wouldst tell me the tale of thy sorrows. Proceed, good youth, and I will not interrupt thee. Art thou the stranger who, but two days since——My voice is choked. But speak; for I will attend to thee."

"I am," now replied Fernandez, with no

no small degree of astonishment at what he saw and heard, " I am that unfortunate stranger to whom doubtless you allude. I am an orphan, whom a few more revolving suns would have seen a happy bridegroom. Yon beauteous maiden, from whom I doubt not you have gathered your intelligence of my wrongs and wretchedness, was my betrothed bride : our hands were joined—our vows were plighted ; she became my affianced bride, and is so still—if she be still in existence. Such was my prospect of happiness ; such was the enviable condition of the now undone Isabel. On my way from the monastery of Montserrat, I was beset by a party of the marauders who infest this mountain : our escort fled, and such as remained were easily overcome. I was taken prisoner, and all the hopes of the forlorn Fernandez were by this cursed chance overthrown."

" Fernandez !" here reiterated the female, softly, but in a hurried tone, as if

the repetition of the name disturbed, and
yet was pleasing to her; " but say, where
dwells thy sire? what is his occupation—
his name—his station in society? Hesitate not, I pray thee! Quick! Oh, tell
me all!"

" Speak with reverence of the dead,"
returned Fernandez, in a distinct but low
and altered tone, which had an instan-
taneous effect in checking the increasing
violence of manner and gesticulation on
the part of his strangely-affected auditor.

" Dead! Is he dead then?" she mournfully articulated, crossing herself reveren-
tially—an action which surprised Fernandez more than any thing he had yet
witnessed. " Is Velasquez de Leon departed? Was it of him you spoke? Is
the husbandman gathered into the vine-
yard of the mighty? Speak!"

" Even so," rejoined Fernandez, with
additional amazement at the interest she
appeared to take in the fate of his unhappy father; and the youth would have
proceeded,

proceeded, had he not been prevented by a loud and involuntary burst of grief from the lips of his singular visitor. She sobbed aloud; she gazed with an expression of wild melancholy upon his youthful countenance, and again veiling her face from observation, by the aid of a tattered portion of her garments, wept audibly for several minutes.

During this paroxysm of mingled sorsow and tenderness, Fernandez stood irresolutely before her, grasping unconsciously the heavy chain that fastened his wrists together, and gazing in mute wonder, not unmixed with a kind of secret veneration, upon the sibyl-resembling form by his side; until finding that the silence was likely to be still further protracted by her excessive emotion, he ventured gently to address her in his turn, desiring to be made acquainted with the cause of her distress, and sympathy with his afflicted situation.

This question, as the interrogator had

E 2   foreseen,

foreseen, effectually aroused Corvetta (for
Corvetta it really was) from the paroxysm
of agony, probably mingled with some
feelings of remorse, into which she had
fallen. She turned her eyes for an instant, full of inexpressible meaning, upon
his anxious countenance, and impressively
replied, in an affectionate tone—" Not
now, not now," said the matron, gravely,
" must that story be revealed, which it
will cost thee many a pang to listen to—
the time is too inopportune, and the place
too dangerous. Observe me then, *my
son,*" she added, with particular emphasis,
" and hold not what I say as light or idle,
but regard it as the assurance of one who
knows well how to plan and to effect a
desperate purpose. It may be long—it
must be long (for I must use much caution in my stratagem) ere we can meet
again; but rest assured, that ere Corvetta
twice shall visit thee, she will have procured for thee the means of release—a
path to liberty; and also for —— But
enough

enough of this at present, we may perhaps be overheard, and a discovery of our
intercourse would render escape hopeless;
so now farewell! Yet despair not, I entreat thee; for as surely as the sun which
sets at eve shall rise to hail the morning,
Corvetta comes again to bring thee joyful
tidings of thy Isabel—to ope thy prison-
door, and bid thee be at liberty. Embrace me once, Fernandez, if thou canst,
and then let us part till thou mayest know
me better. I am not what I seem, nor
what thou thinkest me."

As she made this last request, Fernandez could perceive, by the faint light
which glimmered through the dungeon,
the big tears streaming down her furrow-
ed cheeks; and now approaching the
youth silently, she flung her arms tender-
ly around his form, and ere she released
him, imprinted a fervent kiss upon his
forehead; while as, in the glowing language of the bard—" She pressed his
fettered fingers to her heart," her lips

murmured

murmured some inarticulate sounds, which his ear strove vainly to catch; and hurrying from him, with an expressive gesture, she hastily quitted the dungeon; when, as the door closed heavily after her, and the last ray of light receded from his prison, Fernandez discovered sparkling on his rusty chain—

" The tear most sacred shed for other's pain,
That starts at once, bright, pure from pity's mine,
Already polished by the hand divine."

Now left again in utter darkness, with leisure to ruminate on his miserable situation, Fernandez threw himself once more upon the hard floor of his prison, and began to ponder on the scene he had just witnessed; the final result of which, together with the youth's decision concerning it, must be recorded at a fitter opportunity.

CHAP.

CHAPTER X.

And a magic voice and verse
Hath baptized thee with a curse ;
And a spirit of the air
Hath begirt thee with a snare :
In the wind there is a voice
Shall forbid thee to rejoice ;
And to thee shall night deny
All the quiet of her sky ;
And the day shall have a sun
Which shall make thee wish it done.   BYRON.

THE last peal of the chapel organ had expired among the arched cloisters of the monastery of Montserrat, which announced the termination of midnight vespers; the monks had already quitted the chapel, and were now faintly distinguished in their sable habits

" The cloister-galleries issuing through,
In long, long order, two and two,"

E 4   save

save a few who had not yet risen from
their devotion, having slight penances to
perform, or probably some trivial boon to
solicit of " our lady " and who therefore
remained still kneeling towards her image,
which is formed of carved wood, resembling mahogany, and placed over the altar.
Before this glittering idol, which is magnificently clothed, and adorned with a
crown of jewels, is placed, moreover, a
heap of holy relics, each supposed to be of
peculiar efficacy in the curing of diseases,
mental or bodily; and beneath these precious symbols of superstition and ignorance were prostrated, as aforesaid, several
of the brotherhood, in real or affected humility; but Obando was not amongst
them; his tall forbidding form was not
bowed with the rest in gracious thanks-
giving or humble penitence; neither had
he joined the main body of the monks,
who were proceeding in order to their
cells; but in the distant shadowy part of
the chapel, amid huge columns and hide-
ously-

ously-carved shapes, whose shade served partially to conceal his colossal figure, stalked the despairing malecontent, awaiting with anxiety the disappearance of the few pious members of the convent who yet lingered in the chapel, as if for the express purpose of defeating his intentions.

It was a clear and brilliant night—a night which might have vied with that whereon the guilty, perjured Obando first met the yellow spirit in the chancel of the monastery (since which time, it is necessary to inform the reader, a period of several weeks had now elapsed), and in which fatal interview the overthrow of the monk's remaining scruples was completed, by the insidious proffers of the designing fiend. Through the high and partially-painted casements of the chapel, as on the night alluded to, myriads of bright stars were seen traversing the unclouded firmament; while casting a " dim religious light" around that portion of the

E 5   edifice

edifice already described, as being only indifferently illumined by the holy tapers,

" The moon on the east oriel shone
Through slender shafts of shapely stone,
    By foliaged tracery combined ;
Thou wouldst have thought some fairy's hand,
'Twixt poplars straight, the ozier wand
    In many a freakish knot had twined ;
Then framed a spell, when the work was done,
And changed the willow wreaths to stone."

The marble pavement too, in those dusky
recesses to which Obando had retreated,
was checkered, as on that memorable
occasion, with the mingling hues of flame
and moonshine, which strongly reminded
him of that dreadful eve whereon, by
previous arrangement, as the reader will
recollect, he had summoned the demon to
that terrific conference ; and now their
worship being concluded, such of the fraternity as had hitherto continued in prayer
before the altar, slowly arose, and prepared to retire to their cells. As each of
these, however, passed Obando, on his
way to the dormitory of the convent,
                                        signs

signs of terror were visible in every wrinkled countenance: all crossed themselves as they hurried by, with more than customary precision; and all seemed to regard him with unqualified contempt and abhorrence.

Obando from his dim abiding-place could not but observe this expression of abhorrence, nor avoid remarking the settled aversion which sat on every receding countenance; and as they quitted the chapel, he began as usual to murmur at his destiny, in the following strain.—"Ay, scowl and gibber, ye poor stingless worms!" (such was the muttered tenour of his reflections); "venomless drones, whose poison has been exhausted on yourselves, in the effort by which ye were excluded from society! Your lot is fixed; and by its contemptibleness, your very malignancy is rendered harmless. Yes, gaze on me again," he continued, perceiving that father Jacopo, whose prying and avaricious propensities have been already noticed,

E 6   turned

turned as he quitted the chapel to snatch another glance at his livid features—" in me you behold your superior. Was it not promised me, in return for all I sacrificed, that I should rule abbot over them? Alas! much else was promised too, which I should have valued more; but nothing is yet performed. Am I the dupe of some inferior agent, who cannot fulfil the conditions himself proposed? or——But I am resolved; this night—this very night will I summon him, and compel him to answer for his falsehood, exemplified in the scorn and anguish I still endure."

The remainder of the fraternity, with even the curious father Jacopo, whom it was no rare thing to see last in the chapel, had by this time gained their cells, which they were not likely to leave, until the bell rang for matins about sunrise.

The chapel was totally silent; and even the abbot Ambrose, whose custom it was to see the monks had all retired to

their

their cells, or to grant remittances for such of the brotherhood whose penance might chance at that late hour to remain unfinished, seemed, by the universal stillness which prevailed, to have sought his own apartment for the night.

Now, like an adder from its lurking-place—like a wolf from its shadowy den, or a prowling robber from his daily ambuscade, stepped forth the monk Obando to the celebration of his nocturnal orgies. He advanced towards the chancel : as he drew near, the red cross glared full in his angry countenance, its hues growing deeper every instant. He passed it, however, with a haughty gesture of disdain, and approached the altar. Here pausing, he repeated thrice the talismanic word of " Zatanai !" and with peevish impatience awaited the appearance of the demon.

CHAP.

CHAPTER XI.

"Hail, Satan!" cried he,
"The lord abbot I'll be;
On my bond I demand thy compliance."

English Ballad.

SLOWLY, and as if with a sullen kind of unwillingness, did the yellow-scaled Zatanai appear to the call of his discontented proselyte. At first the burning gleam was alone visible; anon the form of the fiend might have been traced therein, still gathering in intensity and brightness, although not so fast as it had hitherto arrived at its completion: at length the hues grew fiercer—the variable scales became distinguishable in all their fiery lustre and transparency; the head upreared its horrible glowing crest—the visage grew distinct, and the perfect demon stood

stood before him. The earth had not yawned; heaven had showered down no lightnings to create this hideous phantom, and Obando wondered how that which seemed to spring from nothing potent— from pure thin element, could possess the power so to control his destiny, benumb his faculties, and appal his soul.

For some moments the demon looked steadily at Obando, as expecting the monk to begin their conference, by expressing his desire, and the purpose for which he had summoned him; but perceiving that he spoke not (for Obando was not yet so accustomed to the practice of evil, as to be entirely divested of fear when in the presence of a supernatural being), Zatanai sternly addressed him. —" Obando," said the spirit, bending on him a severe look of reproval, " why is the worship of Zatanai neglected? The crucifix is crimson, and yet the hour is past at which thou shouldst have made it pale.

pale. What wouldst thou? Wherefore hast thou brought me here?"

" Spirit," returned Obando, with asperity, although not without some mixture of dread in his demeanour, " spirit, thou knowest my thoughts, knowest too the disappointments I have borne, and the miseries I still am doomed to bear. And canst thou ask me wherefore I now summon thee? Can it be possible thou hast so soon forgotten the covenant wherein thou didst engage to accede to all my wishes, and procure me their enjoyment?"

" I speak not to thee in parables, O. bando," replied the yellow spirit, with an air of sullen indifference, " nor in parables will be answered. If there is aught pertaining to our compact of which thou wouldst complain, speak it with perspicuity—Zatanai will attend to thee."

" Must I then recapitulate my grievances?" whined the monk, in a sorrowful accent, mingled with reproach. " Then, spirit, hear me, and judge if I have not
cause

cause to complain of thee. That damsel,
thou deluding counsellor, whom thou didst
promise solemnly should be mine, yet
holds me at defiance, and spurns my most
alluring proffers with disdain : in vain
have I nightly visited her ; she holds me
in abhorrence, and hesitates not to insult
me with sarcasms on my affected sanctity,
and professions of her attachment to another. My brother I have encountered,
it is true; but there again reality falls
short of expectation : he has hitherto
served me to the full extent of my wishes,
but threatens opposition to them, if I proceed to violence. Thus far, Zatanai,
have I truly related my cause of accusation.   But there is yet another subject on
which I would reproach thee. The fraternity treat me with scorn : they hate,
despise the malecontent; they still pass me
disregarded, or view me as a coiled-up
adder in their path—a reptile to whose
society it were a crime to stoop—a dis-
grace to be levelled. This thou didst
                                   promise

promise should be otherwise. Remembers not Zatanai the crosiered lure with which he won the foolish duped Obando to his toils? I would be abbot: thou hast said it was in thy power to make me so. I would be abbot — principal — superior; I would repose on velvet and on down. Why slumbers then thy potency? thou hearest me."

As the pallid monk concluded, his form seemed dilated with indignation; and his sharp sunken eyes flashed with a radiance which almost equalled the effulgence of the palest of the fiery scales of Zatanai, as if by gazing on him they had acquired a portion of his lustre. The demon grimly smiled at the catalogue of his grievances, and when he had finished, significantly replied—" I hear thee," he responded, " nor needed this recital from thy lips to comprehend thy wretchedness, though bound by holier authorities to demand it of thee. I have heard thee, Obando, and abbot thou shalt be, provided

vided thou shrinkest not from the achievement of the bold deed which alone can make thee so. I am not omnipotent, although my power is great: thou must open thine own path to preferment, monk; I can only second thee, and render the means effectual. With regard to thine other sources of complaint, I have only this to answer—thou hast at present all I promised thee. If he whom thou stylest thy brother approves not thy foul purpose, and refuses to lend thee further aid therein, is Zatanai to blame? and over the inclinations of thy beloved Isabel, I have no control. But wherefore, Obando, dost thou gaze thus wildly down yonder vacant avenue?—Why dost thou shake? and what imports the angry flashing of thy glaring eyeballs? Arouse thee, monk, and if thou wouldst ever win supremacy, if power hath charms for thee, exert thyself to obtain it now!"

Good cause, however, had the guilty Obando to look wild and tremble—good reason

reason was there for his scowling eyes to
flash resentment on the chuckling fiend,
who was luring him, by imperceptible de-
grees, to the vortex of inevitable destruction; for ere yet the yellow demon had
finished his reply, he plainly distinguished
the sound of approaching footsteps, proceeding leisurely along the adjacent aisle.
In a few moments, as Obando had suspected, and doubtless as the demon had
contrived should be the case, appeared the
portly form of the abbot Ambrose, who,
entering at the western extremity of the
chapel, was greeted at once with a full
sight of this cabalistical communion.

Ambrose, on first beholding this unhallowed scene, stopped suddenly opposite to
the arched aisle by which he had entered,
and appeared transmuted to a statue.
Tradition had already made him partially
acquainted with the terrific being before
him; it having been anciently averred
that a spirit of evil origin, and of the same
remarkable colour and aspect, had, from a
remote

remote period, infested their holy cloisters *; but tradition also added, that the aid of the Holy Virgin having been invoked, for the preservation of her favourite edifice from pollution, the spirit had been expelled, and obliged to practise his cabilistical vocations elsewhere. But, however this might be, it is certain the superior was rendered motionless for several minutes, by the excess of horror which pervaded his whole frame, on encountering this hideous and unseemly spectacle.

Meanwhile, on perceiving this confirmation of his worst fears, the monk Obando (who, as already hinted, had from the first imagined the intruder could be no other than the abbot Ambrose, taking his nightly round among the cloisters) stood pierced with terror for his own perilous situation,

* The modern English reader perhaps may smile at this ridiculous supposition; but the existence of such a belief is notorious enough to curious (not sentimental) travellers, among the peasantry of Montrosol, and even some other less renowned parts of Catalonia.

situation, and indignation at the yellow spirit's duplicity, too strong for utterance; Zatanaï at the same time regarding him with a mixture of derision and anxiety, discernible in his fiery countenance.

CHAP-

CHAPTER XII.

Manfred.—I say to thee, retire!
Abbot.—And I reply—
Never till I have battled with this fiend!
What doth he here ?   BYRON.

. . . .

————— ———————Oh, horrible !
The pavement sinks under my feet ! the walls
Spin round !   SHELLEY.

THIS pause of mutual agitation and expectancy was protracted to a considerable space of time, and might have lasted longer (Obando still appearing perfectly stupified with rage and shame), had not the righteous abbot, undepressed by the consciousness of unpardonable criminality, first recovered his reasoning faculties. For Zatanai, potent as he had more than once professed himself, seemed awed like a
" guilty

" guilty thing" in a good man's presence, notwithstanding the sinister expression of his " fire-seamed" aspect, and the undiminished radiance of his burning scales.

As soon as Ambrose had succeeded in shaking off the transitory stupor which had overwhelmed him, and paralyzed like an ague his robust, though not Herculean form, he strove to cast aside at once all symptoms of the fear he had demonstrated, and advanced boldly to the centre of the chapel, as if to assure himself of the identity of the holy brother whom he beheld thus impiously occupied : and then, as if convinced that what he saw was not a mere illusion of the fancy, or, in the words of that truly pathetic bard, and worthy gentleman—" a miscreated mockery of the brain," he, with a steady gait, and an aspect serene, yet dignified, strode slowly towards the chancel.   The form of the yellow demon seemed insensibly to recede, as Ambrose, with " churchman's face professional," majestically approached the

the polluted shrine; while Obando shrunk instinctively from the form of the superior, and bowed his head beneath his penetrating gaze, in secret apprehension, and involuntary acknowledgment of his own misbecoming practices and disgraceful situation.

Ambrose approached the chancel, from which the demon had retired, although without any perceptible motion of his limbs or body; his unison with the elements of which he was compounded seeming to supersede the necessity of corporeal exertion of any kind; and he shrunk from the uplifted cross, sustained by the arm of Ambrose, with the imperceptible velocity of a gliding spirit at the approach of sunrise; while the superior, conjecturing that his triumph over this infernal agent had already begun, and turning towards Obando, with an aspect of severity exclaimed —" Unholy son! (such being the appellation dictated by monastic etiquette, when reproving a member of inferior rank),

VOL. II.   F   knowest

knowest thou to whom thou hast been listening?—knowest thou to whom thou hast this night been bending thy unhallowed conversation?—even unto the evil one—the fell, destructive serpent, whose voice seduced our earliest parents from the path of rectitude, into that of sorrow and iniquity. Sinful son! behold this blessed symbol—embrace it, and avert at least the vengeance of offended Heaven; compared with which, the expiatory death to which the laws of man must doom thee, is but as a grain of dust in the balance." Then addressing the demon, and probably perceiving that Obando was yet too much agitated to notice his exhortation, he continued, in a still more commanding and peremptory strain—" And thou too, most accursed in thine origin, and detestable in thine aspect—thou. who hast too long profaned our holy pile with thy abhorred presence, depart—for thou art. known to me. Depart thou hence, damned spirit, instantly; or by the hatred which. I bear

to

to thee, thou shalt be anon more terrifically exorcised! In the name of our im-
maculate saint, who layeth in the bosom of
the Father, I adjure thee to be gone!"

The yellow spirit grew insensibly paler
during the utterance of these solemn ad
jurations by the holy lips of the abbot of
Montserrat, but did not entirely disappear. His lustre however continued gradually to abate, even after the holy man
had ceased speaking, until the fiery scales,
which at first reflected a brilliant yellow
hue upon the silver cross uplifted by the
abbot, became faded to a shade almost as
livid as that of the precious symbol which
had worked the miraculous alteration.
Whereupon Ambrose, probably conceiving his triumph to be nearly completed,
again turned to the awed and conscience-
stricken Obando, to whom he now spoke
as follows:—" Thou unhappy victim of
depravity," said the abbot—" for such the
incontrovertible evidence of this appalling
scene too surely argues thee—I adjure

thee to repentance. Brief, most unrigh-
teous son, will be, I fear, the term allotted thee to make thy peace with the Heaven thou hast offended. Thou must to
Barcelona, before the holy tribunal* assembled there, to answer for thy enormous
crime: and may He who is all-merciful,
and for which I will nightly pray the in-
tercession of our powerful saint, deem the
sufferings to which thou wilt infallibly be
subjected in this transitory state of existence, by those severer judges, a sufficient
expiation for the offence thou hast committed. Accept this holy symbol, for the
present," he continued, extending towards
Obando his silver crucifix, " which again
let me adjure thee to reverence: the stake
—the public stake, with tortures inde-
scribable, will speedily be thy portion;
and the hour of torment should be pre-
ceded by the hour of pious resignation.
Take

* Of course there could be no holy tribunal near Barcelona at this period, although the Inquisition afterwards
established itself there.

Take it, my son—turn not thus disdain-
fully from the boon I proffer; receive it as
the only consolation which can be afforded thee in thy present unhappy situation
—a consolation of which thou knowest
the value; for however unexampled may
have been thy backslidings (which, alas!
I apprehend are of the deadliest kind), the
Omnipotent, in his clemency, refuseth
none who worship him."

Here Obando, with a sudden wafture
of his hand, and a look of the bitterest
contempt, the only exertion he seemed
yet capable of making, so completely was
he confounded at the probable issue of this
fatal interruption, indicated his refusal of
the proffered token of salvation, and turned towards the supplicating abbot a countenance naturally terrific, but now more
strongly marked with horror and desperation than any he had ever beheld; on
which Ambrose, probably conjecturing,
with some show of reason, that the safest
method of proceeding would be to secure

the malecontent without delay in one of the
dungeons of the monastery, called aloud
to the brotherhood, who were, however,
slumbering much too soundly on their
separate pallets to attend to the requisi-
tion of their superior.—" Ho, there !—
Some aid within ! Jacopo! Jerome !—
Can good men slumber in an hour like
this ?   Awake! arise, Jacopo!   Come
hither, I say !"

While Ambrose was thus engaged,
thoughts of a different nature were beginning to occupy the mind of Obando.
The yellow spirit, Zatanai, it has been
already observed, had faded by this time
to an almost perfect white—albeit his
form still continued visible; and now it
was that Obando, as he began to recover
his faculties, and with them his abhorrence of the abbot (as bad men always
hate that which is in semblance better
than themselves), thought he could distinguish the small shrill voice of the demon much lower than he had ever heard
it

it before, addressing him significantly to the following effect. It could hardly be reality, for Zatanai was at a distance, and the abbot stood between them; yet he fancied he heard something rebuke him for his pusillanimity at the present important opportunity for courage and exertion.—"Obando," it whispered, in seeming remonstrance, rather than reproach, "is a coward! Will he, for the reverence due to a silver bauble, and the arch prate of a designing priest, forego his promised greatness and felicity? Doth he love Ambrose?—That can scarcely be; for the lips of Ambrose betrothed the hand of Isabel to his enemy. Doth Ambrose love him? No; for men give not to the consuming fagot what they love; nor to the rending engine what they desire to preserve unlacerated. Wilt thou burn, Obando? be tortured—massacred? Shall the fiery particles float crackling around thee, and the scorching flames shoot furiously beneath thee? Shall a towering

cloud

cloud envelope thy shorn head, impenetrable as the dubious future to mortal investigation, yet lustrous as the scales of Zatanai? Forbid it, all ye dread attributes of his proselytes! Forbid it, the courage and the wisdom of the worshippers of Zatanai! Obando, strike! lay low yon prattling usurper of thy dignities, and leave the rest to him who has not forsaken thee!"

In an instant the whole demeanour and appearance of Obando became changed. His mien before had been rather abstracted than malignant, and his aspect altogether deplorably dejected—at least since Ambrose had endeavoured to awaken in him a sense of remorse and contrition; but now his keen, rolling eyes again flashed fire, and darted, in a threatening glance, defiance on the intruder. He seemed suddenly to have imbibed a new idea—he surveyed the comely form of the abbot, as if measuring his strength, and inwardly comparing it with his own muscular power,

and

and adroitness in wrestling; for, as neither of the monks were armed, it depended, in case of a contest, solely upon superior force, or agility, which of them should get the victory.

Such were, at the present juncture, the meditations of Obando. Meanwhile, Ambrose, on casting his eyes involuntarily around the chapel, perhaps anxious to discern the approach of the brotherhood, whom he had vainly endeavoured to arouse from the embrace of Morpheus, perceived on the pavement at his feet the impression of a cross, about the size of the crucifix usually worn by the members of the fraternity, apparently traced there by no earthly hand, and which glowed like crimson fire: immediately his eyes darted towards the habit of Obando, and his horror was extreme at finding the crucifix which ought to have depended therefrom was missing; again his form became convulsed with terror, and he franticly exclaimed, looking alternately at the yet vi-

F 5 sible

sible form of Zatanai, and on the monk before him—" Oh! what has here been doing, unhappy man? some fell imposture —some infernal league, to bind thee for aye in the dark trammels of destruction! Speak, thou! who art but human at the worst, and mayest be heard without a prayer for safety, and a bead for pardon— thy fell companion may not.   What hatn been doing here?—why gleams yon ghast- ly symbol, which looks not as stamped there with blood shed in penance, nor glows with the lustre of this middle world? Oh! why speakest thou not? but thy si- lence answers me.   This is no mortal work; thou art the dupe of some infernal artifice, and these the signs that speak thee damned—damned to eternity! for ever cursed!—I know it—I perceive it! Wretch- ed son, lost as thou art, well mightest thou spurn yon sacred emblem from thee! to thee it offers neither hope nor consolation —doomed to everlasting torment———"

Obando could bear no more; the dread- ful

ful veracity of what the abbot had uttered, rushed with double force upon his mind, and a paroxysm of despair and desperation succeeded to his former trance of terror and despondency.   He gnashed his teeth in unavailing rage—he grinned a terrible avowal of his horrible determination to Zatanai; and springing at once upon the unsuspecting Ambrose, fastened him in his gripe, as a ferocious bear would have hugged the devoted object of his appetite or enmity.

For some time the abbot seemed successfully to struggle with his lusty opponent, and neither of the ecclesiastics appeared to have gained any considerable advantage;   but this apparent equality of the wrestlers was only of short duration; the strength of Ambrose was no match for that of his adversary, and it was presently seen, by his gasping and increasing paleness, that he was likely to obtain the worst of the struggle; while the fingers of the pale monk Obando were observed at the

F 6   throat

throat of his antagonist.   A few minutes
terminated the contest; Obando was tri-
umphant; while the imprudent superior
was stretched at his feet, writhing, agonized, and too late repenting of his incautious conduct.

The vociferations of the fallen Ambrose
to his brethren for assistance, it was evident by this time had not reached their
ears, otherwise, although the dormitory
was at a considerable distance, some of
them would doubtless have arrived ere
this; and there appeared no prospect but
of the worthy abbot's speedy destruction,
beneath the fell gripe of his fearful adversary, as, without an especial summons,
none of the brotherhood would, he knew,
enter the chapel before morning vespers,
and he was now incapable of summoning
them thither.

With a visage now black as the sable
garb of his scowling adversary, with quivering limbs, and features convulsed with
agony, lay the expiring Ambrose at the
feet

feet of his successful foe, who still quitted
not his firm and deadly hold of the throat
of his superior. While in this situation,
grappling cruelly with his tortured victim, the malecontent cast his gloomy and
inquiring eyes around the chapel, and perceived on the terrible visage of Zatanai a
grim smile of encouragement; on which he
(scarce knowing what he did) tightened
his firm grasp of the abbot's windpipe,
with the charitable intention of sending
his soul to its eternal habitation as speedily as possible. Meanwhile the starting
eyes of the superior grew dim and glazed,
as from the effect of strangulation—the
blood burst from his nostrils—Ambrose
gasped, shivered, and expired!

But how looked Obando, when he beheld the lifeless body of his first-murdered
victim lying in bloody helplessness before
him? No longer, as the incensed gladi-
ator, did he bend on it a furious and malignant glance, but, appalled and shuddering, shrunk from the contemplation of
what

what he had performed, and, striking his
pale brow with his clenched hand, remained over it in an attitude of intense horror
and stupefaction.

From this appalling spectacle he at
length raised his eyes towards Zatanai,
and discovered, to his surprise, that the
brilliancy of the yellow spirit's scales had
increased again to a degree, which rendered it an almost painful task to gaze on him;
while perceiving the eyes of Obando directed towards him, the demon abruptly
spoke—" Well hast thou wrought, Obando!" he exclaimed, exultingly—" well
hast thou wrought in the cause of Zatanai this night, and well hast thou merited
for it at his hands! Mortal! thou shalt
not lose thy recompence; but the rest of
the task is mine. In the interval, Obando, do my bidding; and as thou lookest
for the future favour of Zatanai, neglect
not again to render him at proper season
the homage he requires, and is from thee,
at least, entitled to receive. Lo! yonder
hateful

hateful cross (for I know it is such, monk,
in thy secret estimation ; but Zatanai desires but outward reverence—to wear the
semblance of evil is to be so) is yet as crimson as thy deeds, and morning must not
shine ere it become as colourless, and void
of bloody tincture, as his whom thou hast
slain.—Fall therefore, fall, and worship
me!"

Obando knelt, as he was enjoined, before the unholy cross, although he knew
not what he uttered, for his mind was bewildered, and his conscience, be it recol-
lected, for the first time, soiled with murder. The demon however spoke much
more at this interview, to repeat which
would notwithstanding be blamable pro-
lixity, as the substance of it must necessarily appear hereafter. Suffice it therefore to observe, that he gave the monk
instructions with regard to the disposal of
the corpse of Ambrose, which he commanded should be left in the chapel, until
found and removed by the fraternity, and
also

also some directions for his future conduct, to all of which his auditor paid, or seemed to pay, the most profound attention. Meanwhile, the wretched Obando still continued prostrate before the long since faded memento of his infamy; his head swam giddily—the walls of the chapel seemed to reel around him—his thoughts succeeded each other unconnectedly and with wild rapidity—confusion appeared to assail him in a thousand different shapes, until memory abandoned its office, and reason found it difficult to keep her throne. In the midst of this chaotic delirium, he raised his eyes to the spot occupied a short time since by his terrible accomplice—but Zatanai was gone.

CHAP.

CHAPTER XIII.

Alas, lost mortal! what with guests like these
Hast thou to do?   I tremble for thy sake.
Why doth he gaze on thee, and thou on him?

BYRON.

Now faintly ascended the voices of the
community, chanting the holy service to
the Virgin, from the chapel of the far-
famed monastery of Montserrat, whence,
sounding deeply on the " dull, drowsy
ears" of its lethargic, tottering inmates, the
bell had some time since announced the
hour of midnight.   The monks were all
assembled, and ranged in order around the
chapel, as already described on a previous
solemn occasion (the demise of Augustine),
and the mass was proceeding in the usual
manner.   The abbot was stalking majestically in the midst of them, with a proud
step

step and an imperious aspect; yet as he
paraded haughtily among the surrounding
brotherhood,

" Though smooth his voice, and calm his general mien,
Still seemed there something he would not have seen"

in the pale, withering glance he often cast
around him, and from which the boldest
of his conventual brethren appeared to
shrink dismayed, whenever it chanced to
light upon their features.

Among the visages of the fraternity,
were discernible those of Jacopo and Geronimo; while in the stern, pale aspect of
the abbot, were distinguishable the gloomy
eyes ,and haggard lineaments of the tall
monk Obando, the despised, deluded
malecontent; with a pensive air, and a forbidding scowl upon his countenance, he
was striding to and fro near the oft-pol-
luted chancel, sometimes shuddering involuntarily, or turning quickly round, as
if pursued by some appalling object, which
it was evident had no existence, except in
his own melancholy imagination. The
holy

holy fathers, it was evident, moreover, still surveyed him with a mixture of horror and detestation; nor did even the meanest of the religious tribe over whom he presided appear, during the celebration of vespers, to regard his superior with looks of complacency, or any other feelings but those created by mingled aversion and contempt.

Meanwhile the abbot Obando (for such he had in reality been created, despite the apparent abhorrence of the brotherhood) continued, wholly disregarding their sentiments, to ruminate, as he walked, upon his dismal situation, which, as it was considerably altered since his last introduction to the reader, and as a considerable length of time had elapsed between that and the present period, must here, with as much conciseness as possible, be further explained.

On the morning which succeeded that dreadful night, for ever memorable to the unhappy malecontent, in conjunction with the other inhabitants of Montserrat's gloomy

gloomy edifice—on which the ill-fated Ambrose was cruelly murdered by the hands of him whom destiny had ordained for his successor, the body of the deceased abbot was found lying in the chapel at sunrise; and no means, or at least no human means, appearing whereby he could have received his death, the brethren failed not (as the demon had predicted, or foreseen would be the case) to impute his decease presently to some supernatural power, such having been well known, at different times, to have infested the cloisters of the monastery. This matter thus disposed of, whereby Obando was freed from all suspicion of the guilty deed, the next important affair to be considered was the election of another superior; and in the adjustment of this second business, as will be speedily seen by their decision, and the grounds on which it was made, they acted with equal wisdom and discernment.

But to proceed without further digression.—The monks were hereupon obliged

to

to elect a new superior, in the selection of whom they had not only themselves to please, as the fortunate candidate accepted (they being all candidates for this post of honour and advantage) must also give satisfaction respecting his abstinence, piety, and other qualifications for the office, to a superior agent of the pope himself, then resident in that country.   This provision then, exclaims the reader, must operate as a barrier to the unjust preferment of an unqualified ecclesiastic to the crosier, or situation alluded to.   Reader, this provision, among the sage brotherhood of Montserrat, was the very insurmountable obstacle which occasioned an unjust conferment of that unenviable dignity, which singular reality is accounted for as follows. —In the choice of their abbot, the brethren were obliged to select for that elevated station, one whose perpetual vigils, and known addiction to severe penances, had entitled him to such promotion, and enabled him the better to endure the fatigues of

of office. This point they were strictly enjoined to attend to by the higher authorities of their holy faith; for the perfect achievement of which they were advised invariably to select for their abbot the strictest disciplinarian, the most resolute hater of enjoyment, in their whole fraternity; and the good brotherhood, however indifferently some of them might relish this austere admonition, dared not act in opposition to such disagreeable counsel, nor venture to do otherwise than as the pope had advised them. Now it chanced that the only member of the convent who could with any prospect of success contend with Obando for the merit of superior self-mortification, was the insignificant father Jacopo, whose avarice and known addiction to cunning practices they even dreaded more than the repulsive and overbearing spirit of Obando; in addition to which weighty reason for rejecting him, the palm awarded for austerity must necessarily be given to the latter, Obando, inasmuch as
several

several of the brethren bore testimony to
his having lately passed whole nights away
from the dormitory, nor once entered his
cell, or tasted the repose (necessary, in their
opinions, only to luxurious and carnal
minds) his pallet proffered him. These
were deemed conclusive arguments in his
favour; for although Obando had once
been suspected of holding evil communion, had not the penance enjoined by a
preceding abbot, in addition to his after
nights of vigilance, and days of torture,
sufficiently expiated his crime?—Accordingly Obando was declared abbot with
little ceremony (the promise of the yellow
demon thus being fully accomplished), and
speedily invested with authority to sway
the crosier over them.

Obando now being abbot, pretended
with much form to exorcise the terrible
spirit from the monastery, by whose accursed power, it was supposed in reality,
by the foolish fraternity, his predecessor
had been deprived of life; during which
hypocritical

hypocritical proceedings, however, Obando sustained his part of affected sanctity, and confidence in the heavenly powers he invoked, very indifferently. For even while he sprinkled the holy essence around him, the gloom of his brow contradicted the phrases uttered by his tongue; and while the name of the exorcising saint was on his lips, the anguish of his heart was incessantly visible on his countenance. About this time, moreover, many masses being said for the purpose of rescuing his immortal spirit from the supposed gripe of the fiend who had terminated his mortal existence, were committed to their mother earth the remains of the unfortunate Ambrose. He was an upright man—and which was more to the brethren of Montserrat, had proved to them a kind and gracious abbot; yet, his body being given unto the dust, and his soul having sought out its abode elsewhere, he was in a short time almost totally forgotten, and his fate remembered only to be narrated to the credulous

credulous traveller, as a marvel and a mystery.

In this manner passed several months, during which the fate of Alfieri de Gracy and Fernandez being unknown, they were concluded dead; as indeed few were known to escape, having fallen into the hands of the lawless bandit Roldan, and his bloodthirsty associates; which, on the arrival of the flying serfs at Barcelona, was instantly reported to be the unfortunate lot of Alfieri de Gracy and his lovely daughter.

Having thus far premised for the information of the reader, we return once more to that important night destined to produce events which materially affected the members of the monastery of Montserrat. The scowl which sat upon the features of the now richly-habited Obando (for although the garb of the abbot was both cumbrous and inelegant, it was splendid compared with the coarse weeds worn by the brotherhood), had by this time gathered to a most forbidding frown of rancour, disappointment, and anticipated revenge. The vespers at length concluded; the brotherhood withdrew as usual, leaving their disconsolate superior to the unmolested enjoyment of his disheartening reflections. For a short time Obando remained motionless in the middle of the chapel, watching, or appearing to watch, the disappearing monks, as they wound slowly towards the dormitory, without seeming in any degree surprised at the visible emotion of their superior, to whose fits of abstraction and melancholy they had become perfectly accustomed; until rousing himself suddenly, he began with furious speed to pace the chancel, often striking his forehead with violence, and sometimes stamping vehemently on the pavement, with all the desperation of madness and despair.

As the last door closed in the distant dormitory, which secured the latest straggler in his cell for the remainder of the night,

night, Obando stopped before the altar, and paused for a single instant in horrid meditation. Then hastening a few steps forward, as if suddenly fired with a resolution which nothing could induce him to abandon, he, with a loud and horrid voice, more resembling the yell of a monster than any thing human, pronounced again the terrible name of " Zatanai!" with a malignant emphasis which made the very aisles around him echo, as if in mockery of his vehemence, the discordant sound.

The monk stood firm, glowing with stifled rage, soon to be wreaked upon the object of his accusation and malignancy. Presently the yellow light shone gradually around—the demon appeared—Zatanai stood before him, for the first time since that fatal night on which the hands of Obando were imbrued in the blood of his predecessor. They regarded each other sternly, and yet differently; in the countenance of Obando was depicted choler,

G 2   almost

almost amounting to fury; while the eyes of the demon flashed living sparks of fire, as if in defiance of his bursting animosity.

CHAP.

CHAPTER XIV.

And arter the league made with him, he shall work deceit-
fully.   *Daniel,* chap. xi verse 23.

THE intention of Obando in thus abruptly
summoning up the demon, was first bitterly to revile him for the internal and
unmitigated anguish he still endured; and
finally to break with him for ever, by re-
nouncing his assistance in whatever future
difficulties he might be doomed to encounter. But when he saw that scaled
and fiery aspect, glowing with an expression of malignancy that far surpassed his
own, his resolution failed him for a moment, and he shrunk appalled from the
superior ferocity of the fiend whose presence he had just before required. This
pause of irresolution was however only
transient; for the demon Zatanai, seem-

G 3   ing

ing to enjoy his consternation, appeared determined not to dissipate the silence; and the abbot was therefore at last constrained to speak, which he effected in a somewhat humbler manner than he had purposed, although with much asperity.— "Zatanai," said he, wrathfully, " thou again hast heard my summons—hear therefore, spirit of darkness, wherefore I have now summoned thee. Five moons have waned—five dreary months have passed away, since Obando became thy willing proselyte; part of thy promises have been indeed fulfilled—but their accomplishment has only tended to complete my wretchedness. I am, alas! so miserable now, that I could madly sue to the meanest of my brethren for that which, unsolicited, I rashly dealt to Ambrose, and fawn upon the hand raised for my destruction. Such are my present feelings, and such is my determination—I am wretched—I am desperate; devise therefore some means for my relief, or in charity destroy me."

"Mortal!"

" Mortal !" replied the yellow spirit, calmly, " all thou hast hitherto required of me has been accomplished for thy gratification. Then whence this weariness of existence ? — wherefore these unmerited reproaches cast on the obedient Zatanai? Thou didst demand supremacy—I have made thee principal: thou didst ask a single interview with thy brother—I have facilitated your nightly intercourse: thou hast possession of the beauteous Isabel— what ails thee at thy happiness ?—but that thou art too cowardly to seize by force what she hath denied to thy supplications. Yet think not that Zatanai cannot even further assist thee. Obando, name what thou wouldst enjoy!—he who influenced the minds of the brethren to elect thee abbot, hath it still in his power (provided thou shrinkest not to perform his bidding) to render thee additional service—and thou shalt find will do so."

" Detested fiend !" exclaimed Obando, incensed beyond bearing at this recapitu-

G 4   lation

lation of the pretended benefits conferred
on him, each of which had proved in
reality an additional curse—" thou hadst
deceived me thrice, ere that last master-
piece of thy infernal treachery!—thrice
hadst thou lured me to the commission of
crime, with promises of enhanced felicity
—kept fatally to the ear, but broken to
the hope. I was ambitious—I demanded
of thee to be made superior, suspecting
not the means thou wouldst select to
create me so: again, thou bloody monitor!
I trusted to thee for the issue of my daring
—and again thou hast deceived me. Tor-
mented with the opposition of Roldan,
the resolute resistance of the high-spirited
Isabel, and the torturing consciousness of
secret guilt, my life is but a burthen to
me—a load of misery too heavy to be borne.
In vain doth the silken couch now court
my fevered limbs, and the silver cross hang
pendent by my side—in vain doth the
crosier glitter in my hand——"

" Wouldst thou rather," said the spirit,
here

here haughtily interrupting him, "wouldst thou rather that keen scourges were flourished in the hands of thy tormentors?— wouldst thou rather the condemned habit adorned, and the flaming pile awaited thee, than the soft couch, and venerated emblem thy predecessors have enjoyed and worn before thee? These, but for the interposition of Zatanai, had each of them been thine—the torturing engine, the fiery stake, and the figured garb of inquisitorial vengeance. But we waste the precious moments that should be more profitably employed: I have never told thee false, however subsequent unforeseen circumstances may have chagrined or perplexed thee: if there is aught beside, in which, as it may be, thou art fearful of proceeding, I am willing to acquaint thee with the means by which it may be accomplished, as bound by the covenant which hath made thee mine. Speak then, Obando—say wherefore hast thou summoned me to this conference? Augustine

G 5   is

is in his grave—Ambrose can trouble thee
no more—the rest, I repeat, is as thou
didst desire: what is it further the obedient Zatanai can aid thee to achieve?"

"Oh! thou art ever ready," cried Obando, impatiently, "to enumerate thy services, or to counsel the perpetration of
additional villany! of which the sole result—too fatally have I proved it—is additional wretchedness. Yes, Zatanai, from
implicit dependence upon thee, I find,
arise only extra repinings and aggravated
misery! but yet, attend to me, while I
divulge to thee once more (for I cannot
restrain the impulse which urges me to do
so) the secret wishes of my soul. My
brother Marco, whom still it irks me to
call Roldan, albeit he answers to no other
appellation, has refused to abet my suit
with Isabel, and has even dared himself
to love the maiden for whom I have imbrued my hands in blood, and subjected
my eternal soul to brimstone everlasting-
ly! When I talk to him of compulsion
—of

—of forcing her to become mine, he prates of honour—says that she is his captive, and must not be used with violence: when I propose her secret removal to the monastery, and aver my intentions of munificently rewarding him for his services, he says no reward can stifle the accusations of his conscience, which would upbraid him perpetually for suffering so much innocence to become the prey of artifice and pollution. Hence am I baffled in every attempt to secure the beauteous prize; and my final success too rendered more than dubious, by his constant protestations of a superior, and yet subdued attachment to the object of my desires. Meanwhile, I adore the fascinating Isabel —I doat on her to distraction!—my hours of privacy are imbittered for the want of her society, and my new state is rendered worthless to me by the lack of her approving smile. Every hour passed away from her appears a century of torment— every moment passed in her presence is

worth

worth an age of supreme felicity. This therefore, Zatanai, do I require of thee: devise some stratagem, however desperate, by which she may become wholly mine, and Obando will be indeed thy worshipper—thy worshipper in spirit, if it be possible, as now in outward reverence, with the mere semblance of what I feel not for thee—so thou wilt vanquish the obduracy of Marco, and bid Isabel be mine!"

In this speech the feelings of Obando had hurried him far beyond what he meant to have said, which Zatanai probably perceiving, took advantage of immediately; and presuming upon this transient rhapsody, in which the monastic had indulged, instigated thereto by the irresistible charms of Isabel, coolly addressed him in the following seductive strain:—" Foolish, misdoubting mortal!" said the spirit, " hath not Zatanai already made thee acquainted with his willingness to serve thee? and needst thou doubt the means by which alone thy desires can be accomplished?

Roldan

Roldan has been thy friend, by assisting thee to effect thy purposes; his threatened opposition to thy will makes him thine enemy. He must therefore be removed; a single blow, thou knowest, procured for thee thy supremacy—a single blow may yet perchance procure thee the enjoyment of this stubborn damsel. Is Isabel of less importance to thee?—are her charms more worthless in thine estimation than the empty rule thou hast obtained thus bloodily?—or is the arm that bowed the struggling Ambrose to the pavement, grown too weak for the achievement of a similar enterprise? Briefly, such is the only course, by a dauntless pursuance of which thou canst with surety reckon on the sole possession of the obdurate Isabel. Roldan is but mortal—resolution and a poniard may easily effect his overthrow: Isabel will then be defenceless, and——but thou regardest me not; rouse thee, Obando!— listen to the voice of Zatanai, and doubt not that he will afford thee consolation."

The

The yellow spirit here cast a grim, tri-umphant look upon the shrinking visage of his distempered auditor, whom he thus hoped to lure to the contemplation of a yet more horrible crime than any he had heretofore perpetrated; and he saw, by the expression of Obando's lineaments, that he was not likely to be disappointed.

CHAP-

CHAPTER XV.

Cain. He is a God.
Adah. ————How knowst thou?
Cain. ————————He speaks like a God.
Adah. ————So did the serpent—and it lied.

BYRON.

OBANDO started at this sudden proposition, which invited him, for a mere momentary gratification, to incur the guilt of fratricide, and appeared for a while completely horror-struck. On a sudden his limbs trembled, his features grew convulsed, and a cold perspiration stood upon his forehead, as at first he recoiled in horror from the appalling project: but these signs of repugnance soon became sensibly diminished, as the demon proceeded with his address, and his aspect assumed a sort of horrid satisfaction at the unnatural proposal,

posal, for which such cogent reasons were in the end administered. This also yield-ed presently to the fixed and stupid stare, which caused the fiend abruptly to break off in the middle of his argument; and Obando heard not the promissory words with which Zatanai had concluded. His eyes were bent in a deep reverie upon the marble pavement of the chancel—his frame now shook no longer—his mind appeared abstracted—he ruminated on the opposi-tion he had already received from Roldan, and the length to which that personage would probably carry his resistance of any other measures than the conciliatory ones found heretofore unavailing. The result of these reflections was unsatisfactory: again he pondered on the probable issue of a desperate contest with his refractory brother, and was again unable to decide to which of the combatants victory was likely to be awarded.

From this confused state of mind, not altogether unpropitious to his purposes,
the

the demon, Zatanai, found it necessary at length to effectually arouse his proselyte; and bending a stern look on him, he accordingly exclaimed—" Obando—awake! —arouse thee, apostate—murderer! shudderest thou at last, renegade and assassin as thou art, to shed the blood of one whose accursed existence is the only obstacle betwixt thee and the attainment of thy wishes? But, be it so; thou art unworthy of the treasure thou hast coveted, who darest not force even a timid maiden to surrender it unto thee. Be it left for a bolder spirit than thine to reap. Roldan, he loves the damsel, and awaits but an opportunity to seize by artifice what has been denied to his supplications, as to thine. Perhaps at this very hour (thou being absent) he puts his design into execution, and wafts her beyond thy reach for ever: this wouldst thou sooner find and know, on thy next visit to the fastness, than by a single effort level this lawless plunderer with the mountain-clod,

and

and end at once his hopes with his existence—Obando, answer me!"

"Mock me not," now replied the somewhat shamed Obando, with much agitation, notwithstanding—" mock me not,
Zatanai, with such a question. Isabel
must be mine: yet tell me, must my passage to her embrace be floated with brother's blood?—is there no other way——"

"There is none," rejoined the demon,
with less acrimony; " Roldan must fall
ere Isabel will be relinquished. And now,
Obando, mark me," he continued, hastily,
having, as he fancied, accomplished his design on the infatuated monk—" for the
first glimmer of the morning is at hand,
and we may commune together no longer:
to-morrow eve, before thy usual hour of
departing from the monastery, repair thou
to the haunt of the banditti; see thou
goest not unarmed; and when, as is thy
custom, thou parleyest with thy brother
in his private chamber——enough! be armed, lest thou repent thy negligence.—
                              Adieu!—

Adieu!—perform thy worship here, ere morning shines upon thee; then hie thee to thy couch. Adieu—adieu!" So saying, Zatanai, more suddenly than he had ever shrunk from view before, began to fade from the vision of Obando; and slowly motioning, while yet his form was visible, towards the glowing cross upon the pavement, instantly disappeared.

The abbot, who perfectly comprehended this departing signal, gazed for a few moments in speechless awe upon the portion of space he had so lately occupied; while, as his fear subsided, all his suppressed choler again mounted into his visage; and turning hastily round, for the purpose of prostrating himself as usual before the unholy cross, he exclaimed, as he eyed the deepening symbol—" Accursed emblem!" said the malecontent, scowling fiercely while he spoke—" hateful, accursed emblem! Oh that I had died ere thou hadst arisen before me, the perpetual memento of my shame—my criminality!—oh that

I could

I could trample thee into nought! Alas! it will never be—thou dost retain, despite my feeble efforts, all thine accustomed brightness; and, except I worship thee, thou wilt never fade. Come then, since ere the bell toll for matins, thou must be obliterated—even must I yield to thee the choice cf the means by which thou wilt be overmastered.—To stab him secretly," he continued, his thoughts reverting suddenly to the demon's counsel, " were an accursed deed—I cannot do it; n r I will not: would I had never been born!"

Thus muttering, the abbot Obando knelt to perform the requisite ceremony, for changing the crucifix from a deep crimson hue to perfect alabaster. While bowed, however, before the infernal sign, his thoughts still wandered from his purpose, and he again appeared bewildered in a labyrinth of fictitious horrors, as on the eve of his last fearful interview with his demoniac adviser. Among other absurdities, equally terrific, and yet ludicrous in
recital,

recital, he fancied the lights placed incessantly before the altar were engaged in
the performance of a mystic dance around
him; while his right hand, which, in the,
heat of desperation, had suffocated the
good abbot Ambrose, led them adroitly
through the mazes of the unholy measure.
From delusions such as these, he arose not
until the grey dawn began to overpower
the sickly streaming of those blessed tapers, and the " soft, warm daylight" warned him to retire with speed to his apartment.

CHAP.

CHAPTER XVI.

Look where he goes, e'en now, out at the portal !
SHAKESPEARE.

ON the evening which succeeded that of the abbot's interview with Zatanai, it chanced that father Geronimo was seated comfortably in the refectory of the convent, by the side of Jacopo, with whom he was indulging a little in social converse upon various topics. Before them was placed a table, it is true; but to their credit be it spoken, the simple fare spread thereon comprised nothing that was forbidden even by the strict rules of monastic abstinence, and self-mortification. A little pure water, in a large brown pitcher, with a small loaf of coarse bread (to which a small portion of dried fish would have been

been an enviable addition), composed the whole of their repast. Over this scanty meal, however, their conversation had been long and earnest; and even, as appeared by the low mysterious tone in which it was still carried on, peculiarly interesting. The rest of the fraternity had successively vanished from the refectory, for the purpose, very probably, of betaking themselves to their pallets, until awakened by the unwelcome sound of the bell for midnight vespers; and the two worthy personages already alluded to were left to discuss, without molestation, the remainder of their subject. As might be supposed, in this solitary *tête-a-tête*, the principal speaker was the garrulous Geronimo, who was seldom so happy as when he could obtain a patient auditor for any length of time; and who, it might with verity be averred, had successively poured his droning narratives into the ears of

" ————— ——————every monk who there
Boasted of piety, but felt despair;

In

In whose dull eyes hope shone not, and whose breath·
Was one unvarying tale of death and death."

It chanced, however, that Jacopo, in the middle of their argument, having ventured a surmise of his own, implying in substance, that men may achieve much (meaning men who are desperate and determined) without the aid of either demons or familiars, Geronimo was heard to remonstrate with him in rather louder accents than he had heretofore ventured to use; and the following was the strain in which he endeavoured to convince his antagonist of the superiority of his own opinion:

" And if, as ye say," replied the loquacious monk, in a tone of eager and triumphant remonstrance—" and if, as ye say, Roldan be not guided in his destructive course by some foul agent of darkness, can ye tell me wherefore his head-gear is perpetually surmounted by that same yellow plume?" (Here his reverend auditor made a sign of inability to answer the proposed question.) " Right well I weened ye could

not

not afore I asked ye," continued Geronimo.
" It is doubtless ordered so, in some infernal compact, by virtue of which (and not,
as thou wouldst aver, owing to his merely
human prowess, or capability to effect such
purposes) this daring man hath intercepted, and holds in the basest bondage, or
slaughters at his pleasure, so many worthy
personages who have visited our convent,
and among the rest the generous cavaliers
who departed hence, accompanied by the
comely maiden of whom you were just
speaking, but who, as our last information
assures us, never arrived at the place of
their destination.   Nor is Roldan the only
personage within the precincts of this
mountain," he added, lowering his voice
again to a whisper, " who has dared to
practise such unholy doings; for, as sure
as there·is wrath in store for the unrighte-
ous man, our most ungracious abbot,
Obando——"

Here the monk was interrupted by another sign from Jacopo, who expressively

intimated his deprecation of any mention being made of Obando.

The loquacious Geronimo however continued, with his accustomed pertinacity in such cases, notwithstanding his auditor's unwillingness to listen to any thing which concerned their superior—" I say our present most ungracious abbot—shake not thy head, man, there are no eavesdroppers here—Heaven hath had little hand in his elevation to that office, which, well thou knowest, good brother, should have been otherwise bestowed (Jacopo nodded a grim assent to this observation) than on such a malignant churl yet such, I repeat, for a limited season, is the power, and such are the works of the evil one and his emissaries. Myself am a godly, striving man, and what, to speak the best of him, hath Obando been more? yet, Heaven preserve us! I say again, Obando is now a crosiered abbot, while I——" and, with a significant shrug, he finished the remainder of his coarse and unsavoury meal.

Before

Before the shrewd Jacopo could return any suitable response, his attention was arrested by a tall, dark figure, which glided past the spacious door of the refectory ; but in which notwithstanding he had no difficulty in recognising the spare, gaunt form of the abbot Obando, of whom his companion had just been holding such imprudent converse. Obando however seemed not to have overheard the subject of their discourse, nor indeed even to have observed the startled brethren, as he hurried by the incautiously expanded portal. His clouded visage (as was customary with him of late) was bent towards the earth, apparently in deep meditation, and his pace, though quick, was exceedingly perturbed and agitated. Jacopo looked aghast for a moment on perceiving him, but presently resumed his former composure; while his companion, who caught the infection later, being naturally more dull of the apprehension even of danger than the sharp-eyed and ready-witted Jacopo, found it more

H 2 difficult

difficult to resume the appearance of his wonted tranquillity. As soon as he had in some degree conquered his surprise, he arose, and motioning significantly to Jacopo, prepared to retire to his cell; nor did the talkative but now-alarmed Geronimo need any further remonstrances on the part of his more prudent companion, to persuade him of the folly of proceeding with his dangerous subject that night.

It was rumoured, however, that on the succeeding day, Geronimo was heard by several of the fraternity, industriously circulating his belief in the surprising ubiquity and other supernatural endowments of the pale abbot Obando; but as this rumour is not authenticated, we dismiss it as an unfounded calumny, calculated to traduce the character of the good old monk scarcely believing ourselves that he was capable of such gross exaggeration and credulity.

To return to Obando. He proceeded onwards, until he arrived at the private
portal

portal already mentioned, which opened to the burying-ground. Having thus gained, unobserved by any one, as he thought, the outside of the monastery, he began hastily to ascend the mountain, too busily occupied in the contemplation of his own vile purposes, to bestow a single thought upon the probable conjectures or conversation of the malignantly inclined, but powerless inmates of the abode he now saw far beneath him. He had lived of late—to use the words of the poet—

> " He trod the world, the spectre of himself,
> Recoiling from the charities of life,
> As chained invisibly to some secret doom ;"

and he now resolved to know at once (like a greater hero in his moment of emergency) " by the worst means, the worst." Accordingly, as directed by the yellow spirit on the night before, he was repairing earlier than usual to the abode of Roldan, not however with the intention of sacrificing his brother—a proposal from which his heart recoiled with horror and aversion,

in proof whereof he resolved to go unarmed, without a defensive weapon of any
kind; therefore he set forth before the hour
of vespers, and, although there was no moon
at this early hour to guide his ascent as
heretofore, soon began to scale the upper
promontories of the mountain.

CHAP-

CHAPTER XVII.

Oh, nature, nature! what can check thy force?
— —   — — — — —
But rush not on destruction; save thyself,
And I am safe. To me they mean no harm,
Thy stay but risks thy precious life in vain.

HOME.

THE moon had not yet risen; the mists
were rolling in huge masses, resembling
to the eye of the traveller mighty volumes
of smoke, among the dusky crags of the
mountain of Montserrat; while the sky
was of a deep azure, studded with a few
pale stars, which, of all the host of heaven,
were alone visible. The different passes
of the mountain were hushed in profound
silence, save where perchance the hoarse
song of the robber sentinel (a proper Phi-
lomel for such a scene) was heard at a distance, as he strove to beguile the " tardy-
gaited"

H 4

gaited" hours of his watch, by this appropriate exercise of his rude voice among the ruder scenery which surrounded him, as, hurrying through the constantly impeding brushwood, was observed a tall female form. conducting by the hand a youth of a gentle mien towards the lower part of the mountain. They were near the bandit's hold, from which indeed they appeared to have escaped, as some remains of fetters were still visible upon the youth's delicate and graceful limbs; while the extreme caution of his conductress, and her evident fear of being intercepted, might well have justified such a supposition.

With slow and deliberate pace, looking round them at almost every instant, did the pair descend over many a dangerous. projecting promontory, towards the rugged post already described, at which was stationed the last sentinel of the banditti. Occasionally, as they clambered downwards, the figures of the fugitives became more perfectly distinguishable, although but

but for a moment; yet even in that single moment the eye of an observer could not have failed to recognise in the female the form of the abused Corvetta, and in the youth that of Fernandez de Leon, the betrothed of Isabel.

With more than redoubled caution they now approached the place where Corvetta knew the last sentinel of the horde to be stationed; and as she yet drew nearer, she discovered a dirk firmly clenched in her right hand, which plainly enough bespoke her resolution. But what was her astonishment on arriving at the dreaded station, to find the pass defenceless, and the sentinel (one of Roldan's most trustworthy guardians, whom she had found it impossible to corrupt from his duty) lying senseless and bleeding at a little distance! Surprised, but not displeased, at this most unaccountable sight, (for who could have thus secretly disabled the faithful and sturdy Gomez?) she paused an instant to survey the prostrate robber, and then significantly

smiling,

smiling, hurried Fernandez forward with increased precipitation.

At the distance however of only a few yards from this fatal post (for fatal it appeared to have proved to him who held it) she stopped abruptly, and seizing Fernandez by the arm, pathetically exclaimed—" There lies the only enemy whom we had in reality to dread!" she cried, pointing back to the fallen sentinel; " that gallant man alone, of all whom I have seduced this night to aid in thy release, did I find it impossible to bribe from his fidelity; and he has met with his reward. Poor Gomez! who would have thought the strength of an unarmed cavalier, and an unpractised peasant, could have overthrown thee!" and as she finished, she dropped a silent tear for the supposed fate of the robber, in admiration of his fidelity, although he had refused to aid her enterprise.

" It seems then," now asked Fernandez, in a hesitating manner—" it seems then,

then, mother, you know who are the per-
petrators of this act of blood?"

"My son, begone!" exclaimed Corvetta, suddenly, without answering his question, as if recalled by the sound of his
voice from her trance of pity over the
wounded sentinel—" there lies your path,
and you will not long lack a guide, and a
companion to render it both pleasant and
easy; go then, and the blessing of all holy
saints, whom it were sin for an outcast like
myself to name, go with thee!"

"And thou," demanded Fernandez, in
astonishment, "my long-lamented mother,
as thou hast partially confessed thyself, and
whom the voice of nature, mingled with
that of gratitude, now speaking powerfully
in my bosom, permits me not to think
otherwise, lies not thy path with mine?
—Thou wilt not tarry longer with these
ruffians?—Oh! flee with thy Fernandez,
despite what thou hast avowed to be thy
purpose, and taste once more the pleasures
of a tranquil and innocent life! for beside

H 6   that,

that, I have further occasion for thee here,"
pointing to the rugged declivities he had
yet to traverse; " it were imprudent now
to leave thee in the fangs of those wolves,
who tore thee from thy dwelling, for even
another hour."

" What dost thou say, my son ?" exclaimed Corvetta, in a sorrowful tone, as if
moved by his appeal to circumstances, and
yet resolving not to yield to it—" what
dost thou say, my son ?—Shall I return to
a course of life which, sooth to speak, I
have almost forgotten how to enjoy ?—
Shall Corvetta abandon those scenes which,
however strange and appalling they may
appear to you, have been endeared to her
by a residence of nearly twenty years ?—
Shall she abandon Roldan ?—No! though
he has proved unkind to her!—Shall she
forsake her mountain habitation ?—No!
though its desolate fragments should fall
and bury her beneath their ruins!—Shall
she return again to a peaceful life—can
she do it ?—No—never! for repose is no
longer

longer an inhabitant of her bosom. Thou hast heard my determination—urge me then no further, but be gone!"

" I go," replied Fernandez, irresolutely —" I go then, but swear by all those saints thou hast invoked in my behalf, that ere another night shall pass, aided by the all-potent Inquisition——"

He would have proceeded; but just then the sound of distant voices, apparently in high debate, caught the listening ears of his wary conductress, and even imperfectly assailed his own. Without uttering a syllable, she again seized his arm, which in the heat of argument she had relinquished, and vainly endeavoured to thrust him forward in silence several times, until finding Fernandez still irresolute, and unwilling to proceed without his second new-found parent, she again exclaimed—" Will it not be?—art thou determined on thine own destruction?— Shall the blood of our true comrade, Gomez, be spilt in vain?—Rash boy ! a moment

ment more, and escape may be prevented. But come, myself will lead a little further: thou knowest not who are chagrined at thy evil-timed delay." So saying, Corvetta once more hurried him forward, proceeding cautiously by his side, along the path which she had before informed him led to the base of the mountain, and they entered a close thicket of brambles and underwood together.

Leaving them therefore to pursue their downward course, we shall proceed to account for the condition in which they had found the wounded Gomez, the real origin of whose disaster Fernandez strove vainly to conjecture, and even Corvetta herself had not conceived.

CHAP.

CHAPTER XVIII.

They found him dead, and cast into the streets,
An empty casket, where the jewel, life,
By some damned hand was robb'd, and ta'en away.
                                    SHAKESPEARE.

OBANDO, as before observed, bent his
course steadily towards the fastness of the
bandit Roldan on his departure from the
monastery ; and as he had by this time
become pretty well practised in the slip-
pery ascent, made considerable progress in
a little time, despite the surrounding darkness, and other impediments which he had
to struggle with, too various to be here
enumerated.   Meanwhile, as he mounted
the now well-known track, he gazed occasionally upon the dew-besprinkled land-
scape beneath him, and the dense clouds
of mist which gathered perpetually around
him, with a look of vacancy that still left
                                    it

it doubtful whether he saw them at all; and then again, " with leaden eye that seeks the ground," proceeded at a brisker rate towards the haunt of the banditti, ruminating doubtless upon the probable issue of his coming interview with Roldan, which he determined should decide his fate.

In this mood he presently arrived at the furthermost outpost of the lawless horde, where, contrary to his expectations, he found he was likely to meet with an obstacle more insurmountable than any he had heretofore encountered. The sentinel was on his post, and with levelled carbine, threatened instant destruction if he advanced one step further, without giving the customary signal.

" Speak the word there, ho!" exclaimed the trusty Gomez, for it was no other; " the word, false monk, or I fire!"

" Hold!" cried Obando, advancing resolutely towards the robber, aware of his having

having seen him often before—" hold! it is a friend—look, and remember me."

" Whoever thou art," returned the marauder, bluntly, " I demand the watchword instantly!" and Gomez again presented his piece.

" I have it not!" exclaimed the startled Obando, but without flinching a jot from the uplifted carbine.

" Then you pass not hence a living man," said the sentinel, who had his own private reasons for suspecting the treachery of the abbot, whom nevertheless he well remembered.

" I had it yesternight!" now suddenly exclaimed Obando; " but circumstances prevented me from visiting this spot; to-day it was doubtless changed; but here is that shall win me a free entrance, if thou art but as wise as thou art daring!" As he spoke, he flung a purse full of Spanish coins at the robber's feet; and, for a moment, awaited the result in silence.

Gomez glanced his eyes downward upon the

the shining treasure; but instantly raising them, with a smile of ineffable meaning on his countenance, proceeded a third time to take a deliberate aim at the man who would tempt him from his duty.

Obando however, probably guessing his design from the expression of his countenance, now hastily prevented him. —" Slave !" cried the irritated superior, striking aside his carbine just as Gomez drew the trigger, which caused the piece to miss fire, " dost thou thirst for murder? —Wouldst thou destroy, like a deluded churl, the abbot of Montserrat, the brother of thy chief?—Thy blood be on thy head then—receive thy recompence !" he continued, fiercely striking the falling Gomez with the heavy part of the carbine, which in the struggle he had wrested from his grasp. Gomez reeled beneath the weight of such an unexpected blow from the muscular arm of the abbot—the crimson tide gushed copiously from his forehead,

head, and he fell prostrate and harmless at
the feet of his antagonist.

Obando surveyed him for a few moments in silence; and then, with a sudden
start of recollection, pensively exclaimed
—" The yellow spirit warned me," he articulated, flinging the carbine to a considerable distance as he spoke—" the yellow spirit warned me not to come hither
unarmed! well, Zatanai, I have disobeyed
thee, and had nearly paid the forfeit. Yet
think not that Obando will ever carry a
poniard to manure these sterile rocks with
the bright blood that warms a brother's
heart: a fratricide! Saint Mary save me!
—pshaw!—saint Devil must be my invo-
cation now! yet, alas! how ill it sounds to
me!"

Thus reflecting, the abbot Obando turned his back upon the fallen Gomez, and
proceeded towards the summit of the
mountain; yet turning once again as he
ascended, with less alacrity than heretofore, he cast a parting glance on the stunned

ned sentinel, as if commiserating his helpless situation. Gomez raised himself feebly at this moment, and applied his bugle
to his lips; but the breath that should have
sounded it was exhausted, and he sank
senseless on the path he had protected with
his blood. Obando saw the movement,
and rejoicing that he was unable to execute his purpose, which might have caused
the monk some difficulty, hastened up the
precipice.

The trivial occurrences which impeded
his further ascent, and the mode by which
he obtained instant access to the presence
of Roldan, affording nothing singular in
their nature, would be uninteresting in
detail. Suffice it therefore to say at present, that the voices which disturbed the
conference of Corvetta and Fernandez,
were those of Roldan and the abbot Obando; but the substance, and issue of their
meeting, must be narrated at length hereafter.

CHAP.

CHAPTER XIX.

All will be well, my Jaqueline—
Oh ! tremble not, but trust in me.
The good are better made by ill,
As odours crushed are sweeter still ;
And gloomy as thy past has been,
Bright shall thy future be.   ROGERS.

FERNANDEZ de Leon now joyfully accompanied Corvetta through several dark
and lonely windings of the thicket, until
they arrived at an open glade, across which
the path they had followed was still visible.   Here she stopped suddenly, although
the impatient stripling would fain have
still proceeded, and looked anxiously
around the small sloping plain, fenced in
on every side with impenetrable brushwood, to which she had conducted him.
Fernandez accordingly paused also; and
following the direction of her eyes, thought
he

he could plainly distinguish several figures
standing beside the very path they were
to pursue, in order to reach the village of
Montrosol.   The cheeks of the youth became blanched at this conviction to a deadly paleness, for he knew himself unarmed;
but the female, with a wild burst of laugh-
ter at his consternation, again hurried him
forward, until they reached the very spot
where the forms were stationed—dark,
motionless, and as silent as themselves.

The foremost of these, a tall, stout
figure, in a dark Spanish habit, Fernandez
now began to think was not altogether un-
familiar to his recollection; and in the next
instant he recognised Alfieri de Gracy.
To cast his eyes eagerly around for Isabel
was his next impulse, and the succeeding
moment beheld the lovely damsel clasped
and almost fainting in his arms.   The
other two (for the figures were four in
number) he presently discovered to be his
former guide, Carlossa, now metamorphosed (in outward semblance at least) to
a marauder

a marauder of the mountain, and the timid attendant of his betrothed bride Inez, to whom the muleteer seemed particularly attentive, and whom all his efforts could hardly prevent from shouting forth her joy at this unexpected liberation.

A transient pause ensued, during which Fernandez (so great was his rapture at this unhoped-for meeting) almost forgot even the presence of his newly-discovered parent, whom nevertheless, as soon as his amazement had in some degree subsided, he thanked with fervency for her services, and the interest she had taken in his happiness; concluding with a repetition of his intentions with regard to the prevention of her future residence with the ferocious Roldan and his bloodthirsty associates.

To this intimation Corvetta impressively replied, while Isabel, with Alfieri de Gracy, and the rest, stood listening in the most profound amazement.—" My son, beware!" she exclaimed, with much solemnity; " I have already cautioned thee

to

to undertake no hostile expedition against Roldan, or his adherents. Beware how thou rejectest a mother's counsel—beware, for thou art in danger, if thou but medi-tatest evil against the horde of the preci-pice of Montserrat! I command thee—I adjure thee, Fernandez, to desist from the contemplation of any attack upon our fast-ness, which could avail thee nothing.—And thou too, stranger," she added, now turn-ing to Alfieri, " for the liberty I gave thee, thou hast requited me by the sacri-fice of the most faithful member of our band : or was it thou, base churl," said she, addressing Carlossa—" was it thou, who, to be revenged of thy former gaoler, hast thus ungratefully repaid my services ?"

Alfieri de Gracy here strongly protest-ed his innocence; while Carlossa, stam-mering in his eagerness to clear up the matter, hastily responded—" Not so, by saint Mary !" cried he, impatiently—" not so, on the veracity of an honourable mule-teer—some time an adherent of cut-throats,

it

it is true, but now about to return to his former honest occupation!—As we approached the pass, we saw Gomez engaged in an encounter with no mortal enemy—though his antagonist wore much the resemblance of that incarnate fiend who, they say, is abbot yonder: but this was a devil—a real devil, by his strength and his adroitness! it was none of our duty to interfere, thou knowest; so we followed thy directions, and luckily enough slipped by them both unheeded. Having reached a little distance, I ventured to turn my head, and saw Gomez lying at the cloven foot of his adversary; on which we hastened forward a second time, but halted in this place, according to the tenour of thy instructions, though freedom lay before us, and the devil drove us on * !"

While yet Carlossa spake, the mind of Corvetta became suddenly smitten with a

"Need must when the devil drives," is a proverb much more commonly used in Spain than (by a certain class) in England.

conviction

conviction of the truth, and she saw the necessity of their hastening to some place of safety. Scarcely waiting, therefore, until he had concluded, she energetically exclaimed—"The monk! the monk!—Obando meanest thou?—it is not yet his hour: but go—begone, while the path is open to ye. Remember, son Fernandez, the adjuration of her who has thus a second time bestowed existence on thee; attempt not to scale these heights, in the frantic pursuance of any hostile enterprise; for such would most assuredly be frustrated. Meanwhile, think of me as one over whose devoted head the tomb hath already closed; for if the wily abbot hath indeed ascended the mountain at this unwonted hour, such, ere many minutes have flown, may be my destiny. Speak not again the time for words is past, and has availed thee nothing: I cannot leave Montserrat: embrace me, and be gone!"

A mute embrace followed this decisive speech, and, hastily waving her hand to the

the rest of the party, she seemed to require their instant disappearance down the
path which she pointed out to them. Alfieri de Gracy, conducting his beauteous
daughter, led the van—Carlossa and Inez
obeyed the signal by following them; and
Fernandez was at last obliged to depart
in mute affliction, though not without
some hope of yet recovering his misguided
parent.

Having watched them disappear, Corvetta now turned slowly back to the aid
of the wounded Gomez, who, although he
had refused to abet her enterprise, or con-
nive in any way at the release of the prisoners, she felt confident had not betrayed
her secret to Roldan, if indeed it had
reached the ears of the chief at all; as
seemed more than probable from the un-
timely visit of his principal confidant in
this affair, the abbot of the monastery.
She found the wretched man still lying
senseless near his station, while the blood
flowed copiously from a wound on his

head,

head, inflicted evidently (despite the shrewd insinuation of Carlossa to the contrary) by some earthly and substantial instrument, such as she well knew the abbot Obando had both skill to wield, and strength to render fatal. Gently she raised him from his uneasy posture, and began, as well as the darkness would permit her, to separate the clotted tresses which concealed his hurt, and to examine its nature. While thus employed, she gradually heard a distinct, yet murmuring sound, arise from the pinnacle inhabited by the robbers, which plainly proved that the fugitives had been missed, and that search was now about to be made for them. Above the rest of the " busy hum," and apparently much nearer to her own station, she could easily distinguish the voices of Roldan and Obando, often raised high in the vehemence of dispute—now uttering mutual threats and imprecations—now sinking again into a lower key, more fit for the expression of irony and reproach. To this

this ominous conference Corvetta listened attentively; but that portion of it which she overheard must be reserved for the succeeding chapter, to be recorded with the rest of the particulars of that eventful interview.

CHAP.

CHAPTER XX.

There's two of you—the devil make a third !

SHAKESPEARE.

FROM the moment of his entering the presence of Roldan, the abbot Obando had displayed a degree of resolution (we might almost have added, of desperation) to which that renowned chief had hitherto believed him a stranger. He demanded that Isabel (such was summarily the nature of his principal resolve) should be instantly delivered to his own private custody, to be dealt with as his clemency or his affection might dictate. This demand Roldan as resolutely resisted, on the ground that she was his captive, and not to be parted with so slightly. Hereupon Obando urged his prior claim to her possession, and

and even offered to ransom her with half
the riches of his convent: but the bandit
was inflexible; he smiled and told him, in
answer to this last proposition, that he
would, whenever he chose, descend and
seize the whole, without asking permission of a defenceless fraternity, or a depraved superior.

Just at this juncture, before intelligence
was brought to the chief of the escape of
Isabel, and the whole of her company,
which otherwise would have speedily
reached his ear, Obando heard the bell of
the distant convent announce the hour of
midnight vespers: instantly he prepared
to depart, requesting Roldan to accompany him a short distance towards the
monastery. The latter consented without
difficulty, and they descended the cliffs
together, their dispute continuing with
unabated violence as they proceeded.—
" Audacious robber!" said the enraged
abbot, indignantly.

" Presuming monk!" retorted the ferocious-looking Roldan, angrily—" monastic hypocrite! dost thou presume to dictate the terms on which the invincible Roldan shall surrender up his captives?   Insolent upstart! where is thine authority?—what power hast thou in readiness to enforce mine acquiescence with thy presumptuous wishes?   Let me but hurl from yonder promontory the smallest of those terrible fragments on thy devoted edifice beneath, and your own devastated altars (I once again remind you) and symbolled walls, covered with brains and gore, will afford you a wide and universal sepulchre.   Be warned, Obando—tempt not Roldan to forget his kindred to the saucy abbot of Montserrat's monastery, I conjure you, as you value your existence!"

" Marco," answered Obando, sneeringly, without however noticing the bandit's threat, on which theme he probably con- sidered it most prudent to be silent— " Marco, thou wert ever a breaker of covenants—a betrayer of the confiding— a violator

a violator of the bonds of consanguinity.
But, Marco, hear me speak; for it may
be, brother, little as thou dreamest it, that
Obando is protected by a power not inferior to thine." Here Roldan interrupted
him with a scornful smile; he thought
Obando alluded to the power of his patron
saint, the holy Virgin; but the abbot, in
reality, implied, as the reader must be
aware, a power of a very different description.—" Was it not stipulated in our compact, that Isabel, the divine Isabel, should
be only mine? Answer me, I entreat
thee."

Even the unblushing, hardened Roldan
felt somewhat abashed at this frank but
ingenious question, which, nevertheless,
he conceived it impossible to evade answering: he knew full well it had been so
stipulated; and he knew equally well that
the conditions ought to have been performed. While however he was preparing
to reply, the attention of both was arrested by a spectacle as singular as it was unexpected.

I 5

expected.   This was the appearance of
Corvetta, ascending the eminence, and
bearing the apparently lifeless body of the
sturdy Gomez in her arms.   Surprised
and startled at the sight, which, at the
best, portended discord among his band,
Roldan stopped and interrogated her;
while Obando appeared to await the result with perfect indifference.

" My faithful Gomez!" exclaimed the
chieftain, recognising with astonishment
the countenance of his fallen comrade,
which Corvetta purposely turned towards
him—" foul play has been used here : tell
me, Corvetta, who hath done this deed?"

Corvetta spoke nothing, but glanced
her eyes, with a significant expression, towards the delinquent Obando.

" The deed was mine," said the abbot,
calmly, almost at the same instant.

" Thine, monk!" retorted Roldan, furiously, surveying him with a threatening
look; " and wherefore hast thou slain my
trusty comrade?"

" He

" He refused to let me pass without the watchword," answered Obando, carelessly —-" he refused to let me pass without the watchword, and thou knowest I had it not.   Had Roldan himself," he added, in a tone of menace, " opposed my passage to the abode of Isabel, he would have fallen likewise."

" He did his duty," replied Roldan, sternly ; " and for thy threat, monk, thou shalt answer this offence with thy life!" So saying, he attempted to seize the monastic, who presently, by dint of superior strength alone, succeeded in loosening himself from his gripe.

" Let me pass to my convent," said Obando, sullenly thrusting him gently aside as he spoke; " it is the hour of vespers, and I must not be absent: let me pass !"

" Vile hypocrite ! thou shalt pass no further!" vociferated the now enraged bandit, springing again with renovated vigour upon the athletic form of the abbot. Obando held him at bay as long as he was able, as a dexterous savage would have avoided the attack of some wild animal; until finding the agility of the robber was likely to prove a match for his own superior strength, they closed finally in an arduous and desperate struggle for the advantage.

CHAP.

CHAPTER XXI.

Now, gallant Saxon! hold thine own.   SCOTT.

. . . .

Howbeit, thank God tis safe. Thank God! for what?
                                            MILMAN.

LONG did these desperadoes continue their
equal contest for superiority, with 'a degree of zeal which not unfrequently threatened the dissolution of both, by a sudden
precipitation over the ledge of an adjoin-
ing promontory, to the very brink of which
their struggle had conducted them. It
was during this trial of strength, which
it seemed probable would terminate in the
destruction of at least one of the parties,
that Gomez gave some feeble signs of returning life. Accordingly, Corvetta, on
perceiving that a faint palpitation yet lingered in the body of her charge, again
                                        addressed

addressed herself to the task of dragging him up the promontories, leaving Roldan to deal with his antagonist; for, as Corvetta really believed that chief to be invincible, she had little fear for the result; concluding of course that it would be in his favour. She therefore proceeded upward with the insensible Gomez, whose quivering lips now uttered a low moan, as if in thankfulness for her attention.

No sooner was she out of sight, than the strength of the abbot Obando began gradually to get the better of his adversary's activity and skill in wrestling. Roldan, who now felt himself about to be overpowered, searched his belt vainly for his trusty hanger: it had fallen off during the struggle, and was now lying at a considerable distance. In this dilemma, he suddenly thrust his hand into his bosom, and drawing forth a poniard, would have speedily terminated the career and crimes of his antagonist; but being by the effort thrown off his guard for a moment, Obando

do took the advantage thus proffered him by his adversary's treachery ; and, with a dexterous movement of his body, stretched the daring marauder prostrate at his feet.

Roldan however fell not so suddenly as to prevent his drawing into view the concealed poniard, with which it was evident he had meant to

> " Set abroach the blood that should have flowed
> In calm and natural current"—

his brother's blood—the blood of the abbot of Montserrat, whose predecessor that very poniard had assisted to massacre near the bloody pool. Obando accordingly saw the weapon ; and as the chieftain was now entirely at his mercy, found little difficulty in wresting it from his grasp, thus becoming himself master of the blade bared for his destruction, on which, brandishing it triumphantly over the body of the fallen leader, he gnashed his teeth furiously, and exclaimed, with deep but suppressed emotion—" Curses on thee !" muttered

tered Obando, shaking his victim violently
by the collar of his armour—" curses on
thee! the fate of all who have been Obando's enemies be thy bitter portion!"   Yet
he delayed to strike: it was his brother's
eye that now looked up to him for clemency—it was his brother's form that lay
prostrate at his feet.   Obando was not entirely abandoned even yet by the finer
feelings of his boyhood; and hurling the
dagger to a considerable distance, it struck
against the edge of a projecting promontory with a force that shivered it to splin-
ters—" Rise—for I cannot slay thee!" now
shouted the agonized Obando, with somewhat less vehemence than heretofore; but
first acknowledge that Isabel de Gracy is
destined for——"

" Not for thee!" articulated Roldan,
faintly, and yet in a determined tone.

The patience of Obando could bear no
more; with a single spurn of his foot did
he send the prostrate form of his brother
rolling over the ledge of the aforesaid promontory,

montory, whence it bounded apparently, rustling over weeds and brushwood, into the gulf below. The abbot watched it proceed from rise to rise (for luckily the descent was not quite perpendicular) until it had reached a considerable distance, in the attitude of a man transformed to stone. He shuddered at what he had done—his blood retreated to his heart—his forehead, flushed before with exercise, grew paler than the purest marble. Suddenly he seemed to recollect himself: the body had disappeared from his strained vision, and it seemed probable no human eye would ever more encounter it. He tore himself away, and, in a state of mind closely bordering on distraction, sought out the path which would conduct him to his monastery.

As Obando descended the mountain hastily towards his convent, the moon rose slowly over a projecting point of the mountain, and her beams burst gradually through the clouds of vapour, which at every angle where water presented itself, still

still continued to envelope him.   The bell
for vespers still continued moreover to
peal harshly in his ears; for the absence of
their abbot had somewhat alarmed the timorous fraternity, and they therefore kept
it tolling for a longer period than usual.
Anxiously, as he descended, did he gaze
around him, in the hope of discerning
some trace of the body of Roldan—but in
vain; all was lonely—all was silent; and
Obando ventured not to call, lest his voice
being heard by the brotherhood, should
betray the point to which his midnight
stroll had been directed.

At length he reached the level tract of
ground on which the convent was situated,
and pausing here awhile to recover his
breath, he could not avoid taking once
more a cursory survey of the rude and
magnificent scenery left behind him.

The bell had ceased to toll, the moon
was beginning to spangle the declivity of
the mountain, and all, except the bosom
of the abbot, seemed to partake of the universal

versal tranquillity which pervaded the
scene.   On a sudden he thought he heard
a distant murmur, as of several voices loudly exerted, which appeared to proceed
from the upper part of the mountain and
accordingly straining his eyes in that direction, he plainly distinguished several
groups of figures carrying lighted torches
in their hands (which the faintness of the
moonshine yet rendered necessary), de-
scending towards the spot of his late encounter with the treacherous Roldan.
These he doubted not were parties of the
banditti in search of their chief, of whose
danger the indefatigable Corvetta must
already have apprized them; and in this
conjecture he was presently confirmed, by
the following proof of its being well
grounded.

While yet the abbot was gazing towards the gathering swarm of banditti,
whose forms at each succeeding instant
became more distinctly visible, the murmur of voices considerably increased; and
he

he could, as they drew nearer, easily recognise the hoarse voice of Sebastian, mingled with the rest, calling loudly upon their hapless leader. Obando listened still, and presently thought he could distinguish a faint cry proceeding from a lower part of the eminence they occupied, as if uttered in answer to their clamorous salutations. In a moment all was profound silence; and now again the feeble shout distinctly reached his ear, and also the ears of the robbers; for they instantly made, with one accord, towards the spot from whence it issued, which Obando knew to be the very glen into which he had rashly precipitated the form of their chief, and where, had the body as it rolled downward chanced to take an opposite direction, it would inevitably have been dashed into a thousand atoms.

"Praised be Heaven, he lives! he lives!" murmured the abbot, with apparent fervency; then, as he turned to enter his monastery—"Praised I heaven?" he continued,

tinued, gloomily: " what have I to do
with heaven?—the heaven for which I
bartered my salvation was but a piece of
painted frippery, and even of that I have
been disappointed!"

Thus musing, he proceeded to the private door already so often mentioned in
this narrative; and having opened it,
turned once again to ascertain the further
progress of the horde in the discovery of
their leader: an unbroken stillness prevailed over the late scene of uproar, while
a few were observed slowly reascending
the mountain, with their torches extinguished, a sufficient proof that they had
effected the purpose for which they had
been illumined.

CHAP.

CHAPTER XXII.

Deep, from that melancholy pile,
  The bells at eve are swinging ;
And lights are seen in the cloistered aisle,
  For the convent mass is singing.   BASIL.

VESPERS had commenced long ere the
abbot Obando entered the chapel appropriated for their celebration ; but when he
did so, it was with a steady gait, and an
unmoved, though sorrowful aspect, as
from the infliction of some secret penance,
or self-imposed discipline—such power had
habit given this unhappy being of con-
trolling the violent emotions of his trou-
bled spirit. Not long, however, did he
on the present occasion preserve this se-
date and hypocritical demeanour; for soon,
too soon, his features became contracted
into more than their accustomed harshness;

ness; while the involuntary scowl upon
his haughty brow, and the frequent flashing of his fiery eyes, betrayed the incessant workings of his soul. He strode to
his appointed station near the chancel, on
his entrance; and notwithstanding the evident perturbation of his mind, joined in
the holy ceremony, though his " brain
was whirling giddily, and his heart was
scorched with fire."

It is needless to observe, that the parti-
cipation of Obando in the sacred worship
of the brotherhood was only mechanical,
therefore a mere outward show of reverence to the Deity which he did not feel.
His thoughts were in reality far otherwise
employed; he was contemplating the risk
he had encountered in thus provoking the
resentment of the fiery-spirited Roldan,
against whose dreaded vengeance he now
doubted whether even the power of Zatanai could shield him. Isabel too he began to be apprehensive, was now lost to
him for ever: for how could he attempt
to

to recover her? To venture again among the horde of Roldan, would be to encounter certain destruction; for how zealously would those ruffians avenge the quarrel of their leader, especially upon one of Obando's detested habit and calling! This consideration induced him speedily to abandon the idea of ascending the mountain, or even quitting the convent again alone. How then was he to obtain possession of the beauteous prize, for whom he had sacrificed his tranquillity in this world—his hope of salvation hereafter? He knew not, nor could conceive any mode of procedure which promised the least chance of success to his exertions; and this conviction added considerably to his natural gloom of aspect, and rendered him an object of terror and detestation.

While buried in these despairing ruminations, yet instinctively, as it were, performing among the assembled brotherhood the duties of his office, the ears of all present were assailed by a loud rumbling noise,

noise, as of thunder pealing in the welkin just over their devoted heads. Scarcely had they recovered from the amazement excited by this unlooked-for phenomenon, ere a second crash, more dreadful in its effects than the former, burst furiously over them; that instant the carved and gilded ceiling of the chapel was separated, and through the yawning aperture descended a huge fragment of stone of enor mous magnitude. This appearance at once explained the cause of their terror, but allayed it not: the affrighted brotherhood, who, on the first shock, suspected with some reason that the day of doom was arrived, now hurried up and down the chapel, in yet wilder disorder and dismay—so terrible to them in idea was the execution of Roldan's often threatened vengeance. Some flung themselves in humble supplication before the yet-uninjured altar, in the vain hope of averting their doom by prayer; while a few fled, at the first onset, to the solitude and temporary security of their cells. Geronimo dropped on his knees in the place where he was standing, and with hands which trembled with age and apprehension, be, gan, for the last time, as he feared, to fumble over his rosary—an example in which he was followed by many of his equally timorous brethren, whose dread of Roldan was, like his own, almost equal to the antipathy they professed towards Sa-tan himself.

It should here be briefly remarked, in common justice to the individual, that he who amid this tumultuous consternation seemed most ably to preserve his self-possession, and power of acting on the defensive, was father Jacopo. He steadily watched the countenance of the abbot, as if expecting him to issue some command respecting the conduct to be adopted in this exigence; and whatever that com-mand might be, father Jacopo seemed de-termined to fulfil it, if its execution was found practicable. But where was Oban-do?—

do?—how brooked he this disastrous commencement of the hostilities which he
alone knew they had good cause to apprehend? Reader, your curiosity shall be
speedily gratified. The abbot was standing, pale and motionless, beside the fallen
fragment—a spot from which he had never stirred since the first cause of alarm
was audible. The brethren had actually
mistaken the first assault, which, as already narrated, failed to perforate the roof
of the edifice, for a loud clap of thunder,
the prelude to a sudden tempest; but
Obando, who knew the species of thunder
they had most to apprehend, was not so
easily mistaken: he well knew that the
hoarse battering above him could only be
occasioned by the dreadful ammunition of
those whom he had been imprudent enough
to make his enemies; but he also knew
that defence would be unavailing, as the
descent of the second mass sufficiently
proved to the conviction of every quaking
inhabitant of that devoted pile. The holy

K 2   service

service was now suspended, and should that infernal mode of assault be renewed, it seemed more than probable that the whole monastery would, before the morning, be a demolished heap of ruins. Thus situated, as a last and desperate expedient, the abbot determined to summon Zatanai to his succour and counsel; which resolution had no sooner been taken, than he prepared as suddenly to execute it. Accordingly, with an imperious wafture of his hand, he commanded the brethren to their cells, bidding them there employ themselves in prayer, as every other species of defence would now avail them nothing. This order, although deemed somewhat injudicious by Jacopo, was readily obeyed, and Obando remained alone in the chapel.

CHAP·

CHAPTER XXIII

Come with a word—I thank thee—Ariel! come.
                                    SHAKESPEARE.

ON finding himself unobserved, the unfortunate abbot strode hastily several times
across the chapel, as if considering in what
strain he should address the inexplicable
being whom he was about to summon.
At length rage predominated over every
other consideration; and with a visage
now rendered frightful indeed by those
violent, conflicting emotions which it still
essayed to hide, he furiously advanced towards the chancel.   It was now that solemn hour, aptly defined by the immortal
Shakespeare, as—

" ———the very witching time of night,
When churchyards yawn, and hell itself breathes out
Contagion to this world;"

and who that saw the agonized and incensed Obando at that terrible moment, but would have believed him a " native of another and worse world?" and, to conclude, who would not have exclaimed with the wondering Caloyer—

" If ever evil angel bore
The form of mortal, such he wore:
By all my hopes of sins forgiven,
Such looks are not of earth nor heaven!"

Thus wound up to the highest pitch of frenzy, by a contemplation of the various circumstances, which seemed to conspire against him as if preordained by that malignant phantom for his destruction, the most unholy abbot Montserrat ever witnessed within its sanctified precincts, proceeded to call up his infernal auxiliary to his assistance in this dilemma—" Zatanai, thou most accursed deceiver! (it was thus he reviled the spirit he was necessitated again to invoke) appear!—arise—appear, false demon as thou art, thou darest not evade

evade the summons of Obando.   Appear, I say—appear !"

Slowly, and with seeming unwillingness, but much real gratification, did the yellow fiend appear to the call of the abbot as heretofore.   The conduct of the demon, Obando had before remarked, seemed of late to be entirely changed; since, willing as he was formerly to arise in the presence of Obando, even without any direct solicitation, he now came reluctantly to his repeated summons, and was ever foremost to break off the interview.   Howbeit, he at length stood once more beside his proselyte, in all his former imposing, but (to Obando) no longer alarming brilliancy; and the abbot, in spite of the hatred he bore to the object before him, could not avoid inwardly testifying his unwilling admiration; for never had he beheld the fiery scales of Zatanai burn so brightly and so beautifully as at that moment.

" Zatanai, the Philistines are upon me !"

now

now cried the abbot impatiently, without waiting for the address of the demon, and profaning the language of scripture in his own, " they have broken my stronghold, even as thou seest, and I am in their power. Say, spirit, is this the promised recompence of my sworn fealty to thee?—this the reward of my misdirected prayers—my sacrifices of eternal weal, for everlasting misery? Deluding fiend, speak!—wherefore, in mine extremity, hast thou thus deserted me? and why am I delivered into the hands of mine enemies? for soon will Roldan force our rotten gates, rendered by time too weak to resist his entrance, and soon will the wretched Obando become his victim."

The demon scowled yet more terrifically as Obando concluded, but returned no other answer; on which the distressed abbot resumed—" Why, demon, art thou silent?" he continued, in the same strain of mingled reproach and supplication.— " Isabel too thou didst promise should be mine—yet Isabel will now be another's:

couches

couches of down didst promise for my repose—but, alas! I can rest on them no
longer: costlier garments than I was wont
to wear hast thou bestowed upon me—
but they clothe not the bosom of peace,
nor can for a single moment assuage the
inexpressible anguish which devours me.
Thou didst promise me, moreover, thine
assistance in mine hour of peril, or of adversity; speak then, for I am in danger;
and when was the betrayer a niggard of
his treacherous counsel? Speak, Zatanai!
how shall I avoid the destiny which now
threatens me?"

" Frail, erring mortal!" at length responded Zatanai, without softening the
stern gaze with which he regarded his
devoted proselyte, or betraying any symp-
tom of commiseration for his plight—
" frail, erring mortal! who hast neither
the inclination to perform good actions,
nor the courage requisite to work evil
ones! hadst thou obeyed the dictates of
Zatanai, thou hadst not now needed his

advice

advice to extricate thee from the web of inauspicious incidents, thou hast, by neglecting it, permitted thine enemies to wreath around thee. Thou art environed on every side, although thou knowest it not, by deadly enemies, who were never yet defeated, or foiled in their infernal machinations. Accuse not me as the author of thy calamities; my advice, I repeat, if followed, would probably have prevented their existence. Did I not warn thee, Obando, yesternight, that Roldan must perish ere thy wishes could be accomplished? Now, answer me—hast thou done thy best endeavour to effect his overthrow?—hast thou not rather, fickle-minded coward! hast thou not rather tendered his existence as a thing precious to thee, than attempted to deprive him of it? Answer me faithfully, as thou wouldst obtain my future services. Why dost thou shrink, and turn aside thy visage? Obando I command thee, answer me!"

" It would be vain to attempt deceiving thee,"

thee," now sullenly responded Obando,
after an irresolute pause; " I brandished
a poniard over his prostrate form—I flung
the weapon from me—I could not take
his life."

" And in sparing it thou hast endan-
gered, perhaps sacrificed, thine own," rejoined the demon significantly, with a
fierce, yet somewhat meliorated glance of
displeasure; " he would have deprived
thee of existence, wherefore shouldst thou
hesitate to requite him with the doom he
meant for thee?   To have sheathed that
poniard in his body who drew it against
thine, would have been only to commit
a deed which prudence must have ap-
plauded, and justice would have sanction-
ed.   Hear me, Obando," he continued—
" hear me; for dastardly as thou hast de-
meaned thyself this night, I will yet be-
friend thee; since those are still disciples
of Zatanai, who, possessing the wish to
work evil actions, are yet deficient in the
spirit so necessary for their execution;

and such a knave art thou, whose heart dares brood over ill deeds thy hand hath shrunk from the perpetration of. Some events have happened yonder with which thou art yet unacquainted; these Zatanai will narrate to thee, and then choose whether thou wilt abide their consequence in this place, or away with me to an abode thou wottest not of, there to reiterate thy solemn professions of fealty, and, finally, to abide with Zatanai for ever!"

Here the yellow spirit narrated briefly to the tortured and astonished Obando the escape of Isabel from the power of Roldan, with some subsequent circumstances of an appalling kind, with which the reader also is not yet acquainted: the principal of these was the meeting of Fernandez and Alfieri de Gracy with a strong party of inquisitors, who were crossing the mountain in search of a suspected victim of the Holy Tribunal: these he easily induced to listen to his fervent depositions against the abbot Obando,
whom

whom he accused of the practice of almost every enormous crime; for these officers are like bloodhounds, and, in the polished language of the refined Milman,

" When the tale is rife
With blood and desolation, then, oh ! then
They listen with a cold, insatiate thirst ;"

although, to the " plea of mercy," they are too often stones indeed. Finally, he had succeeded so well, that the officials had resolved to consign the accused Oban-do to their dungeons at Barcelona; and, as the yellow spirit asserted, while Roldan was advancing against one side of the monastery, resolved on the destruction of its abbot, a power from the terrible Inquisition, aided by Fernandez and the peasantry of the neighbourhood, was ready to assail it on the other.

CHAP-

CHAPTER XXIV.

Obando chose that course which seemed to proffer him the
greatest advantages.

History of Columbus.

OBANDO listened to these tidings with inexpressible horror, confusion, and dismay;
he dreaded death much, as the terrible
hereafter to which he had consigned his
immortal soul now rushed upon his memory; but the Inquisition—that terrible
tribunal which tortured its victims into a
full confession, and afterwards burnt them
for their iniquities, he dreaded still more.
In this dilemma, he saw no possible prospect of escape, except by complying instantly with the last proposal of the yellow demon; and how was he then to be
rescued?—Which way was he to obtain
egress, since both sides of the monastery
were

were beset with irreconcilable enemies? Might not Zatanai have deceived him ?— No, for the assault of Roldan not having been renewed from his impregnable battlements, he made no doubt of that chief having now descended with his comrades, in order to force open and search the convent for the fugitive Isabel, for whose sake, it now seemed probable, he had for a while delayed its demolition. Thus circumstanced, he knew not what decision to make; but stood trembling and distracted, his pale lips quivering with rage and apprehension, until the demon once more reminded him of the necessity of forming a speedy determination.

" Choose !" exclaimed the exulting Zatanai, whose greaved, transparent covering was never so brilliant as now—" choose ! Wilt thou begone with Zatanai, far—far beyond the reach of thine inveterate enemies, or wilt thou stay, and perish by the ruthless combination which thou seest is forming against thee ?—Our time is brief —decide,

—decide, or thy decision may yet avail thee nothing! for however Zatanai may scoff at the hypocritical sanctity of those pretenders to holiness who are approach. ing, they bear that with them which I may not look upon; the blazoned symbol of their perverted faith gleams in the van of their array, and ere its entrance here, must Zatanai perforce forsake thee! Speak then—decide, I say!—Which wilt thou do?"

Obando, amid the chaotic recollections and surmises of that horrible moment, was yet unable to make any distinct answer. At length, however, rather speaking what was uppermost in his mind, than making any direct proposition to which he ex- pected the demon would agree, he fran- ticly exclaimed—" What if I fling myself humbly at the feet of Roldan—entreat him to pardon my precipitance, and sup- plicate his protection?" he articulated, in a tone of self-interrogating perplexity— self-accusing desperation and despair.

" And

" And by an act so rash," returned the yellow spirit, readily replying to the question which was but half intended for his ear, " accelerate thy destruction!—Expect not clemency from the marauder of Montserrat, Obando; such mercy as the wolf robbed of his food by stratagem, would yield, even such shalt thou receive at the hands of Roldan. Methinks I already see his poniard hilt deep in thy bosom, thyself unarmed, and powerless at his feet—I behold the laugh of exultation triumph in the features of his brutal followers—the languor of death succeed the flush created by false expectation on thy countenance—the red stream bubbling down——"

" Suppose I cast aside this hateful garb and endeavour to save myself by flight?" now rejoined the abbot, interrupting him, as if sickened at the picture he was drawing of the triumph of his lawless assailants—the despised banditti.

" And meet the officials of the Holy Tribunal," retorted the demon, angrily, with
a mixture

a mixture of scorn and derision in his aspect, " who know too well their duty, and are much too deeply skilled in the hellish practices of their cruel occupation, to suffer their prey to escape them so easily. How wilt thou endure their torments, their racks, their screws, their agonizing cords, and crooked engines of torture, when suspended over some accursed machine, thy cramped joints forsake their shuddering sockets, or stretched beneath their burning pincers, thy straining eyeballs glare with wild amazement? and then at last the foul close of tyranny—the condemned habit, figured all over with the emblems of thine infamy—the scorching, fiery pile —the bright, curled flames around thee, hissing—crackling—mounting——"

" Fiend, forbear!" now cried the distracted abbot, who saw but too much probability of this description being realized— " mock not thus the misery thou hast caused! How shall I shun—what shall I do to avert this horrible destiny?"

" Be

" Be mine !" rejoined the now victorious demon—victorious, at least, in his own vile conjectures—" resign thyself to me—thy body to my guidance—thy soul to my eternal keeping, so shalt thou be delivered—Zatanai will deliver thee! swifter than thought shalt thou be borne afar from peril, where neither holy symbols, nor divine missionaries, shall affright thy spirit more !"

" Whither wilt thou bear me ?" was on the lips of Obando, when a sudden alarm of firearms without the portal of the monastery prevented his utterance of the question. This was occasioned by the arrival of Roldan, and a numerous party of the banditti, at the private portal of the convent, against which, as an intimation of their intentions, or more probably to assay the strength or thickness thereof, a few of them had discharged their arms. In a few moments was heard a loud rumbling sound, as of something applied to the door in order to force it open, which operation, accompanied by a general shout from

from the rude throats of the robbers, min-gled, as it died away, with threats and ex-ecrations, commenced presently. Furi-ously did the clatter now continue at the private, and consequently the weakest, door of the monastery; for Roldan felt assured that Isabel had 'n reality escaped by some treachery of his brother Obando, and was doubtless concealed in the con-vent; a supposition which proved fortunate enough for the inmates of Montserrat, which otherwise the formidable destructive stones of the banditti would have battered without mercy to the ground.

Just at this instant too, on the front or larger portal of the monastery, was heard, distinguishable above the adjacent uproar, the solemn knock, thrice repeated, which announced the approach of the officials of the Inquisition. Obando started back in unaffected horror—it was a moment of in-tense anxiety.

" Dost thou resign thyself to me—thy
soul

soul to my eternal keeping?" again demanded Zatanai, impatiently.

" I do! I do!" sobbed forth Obando,
wringing his hands in an agony of terror;
" but——"

The meditated objection of the monastic, it appeared, came too late; for that instant Zatanai advancing, laid his hand (or
what resembled such) lightly upon his
shoulder. Obando felt himself immediately uplifted from the ground, and trans-
ported, with his horrible conductor, through
the already-mentioned aperture made by
the falling fragment in the ceiling of the
monastery. Their motion was not swift
—no cessation of the breath accompanied
it; but the awe of his situation transfixed
Obando in silence, while a sickening sensation crept over his whole frame, and his
looks were as the aspect of one who would
never speak again!

Just at this moment, the whole body of
the brotherhood, who knew the signal,
and conceived themselves unquestionably
bound

bound to admit the officers of the Holy Tribunal under any circumstances, rushed tumultuously into the chapel. To describe their astonishment at the spectacle which presented itself would be impossible; each was truly in the situation of him in Scripture, who exclaims—" I have heard of thee by the hearing of the ear; but now mine eye seeth thee." Meanwhile Obando, accompanied by his luminous companion, issued majestically through the chasm aforesaid, and appeared to ascend the loftier vaulted firmament.

CHAP.

CHAPTER XXV.

Cain.   I tread on air, and sink not! yet I fear
To sink.
    Lucifer. ———Have faith in me, and thou shalt be
Borne on the air, of which I am the prince.
    Cain.   Can I do so without impiety?

BYRON.

BUOYED up in middle air by the preter-
natural agency of his conductor, high above
its loftiest pinnacle, Obando surveyed with
a wild, stupid stare the succession of events
which took place in the monastery beneath him.   He perceived that the robbers, finding every other mode of obtain-
ing an entrance ineffectual, had set fire to
the convent towards that angle where the
private door was situated; and that already
the clear flame was ascending to the upper rafters of the edifice, so dexterously
used had been their innumerable torches,
                                            while

while a huge column of black smoke began to aspire towards his own elevated situation, a further proof of the rapid progress making by the destructive element. On the other side, opposite the front gate of the monastery, he could distinctly perceive the dark forms of the officials, bearing with them, as Zatanai had predicted, the holy standard of the Inquisition, over which now the ruddy, aspiring flame, that burst forth on the opposite side of the building, began faintly to diffuse a horrible and portentous lustre. In a few moments the emissaries of the Holy Tribunal were admitted by the brotherhood; and almost at the same instant (utterly ignorant as yet of the formidable foes they had there to encounter, imagining the monastery to be, as usual, merely the receptacle of unarmed monks and pilgrims) did Roldan and his outrageous followers gain entrance by means of the ruin they had effected in another quarter of the edifice.

The flame created by these bold incendiaries

diaries had by this time increased to a spiral blaze, which peered above the .top of the monastery, and illumined the cross of skulls, erected over its site, with a terrible radiance, which, reflected by so ghastly an object, caused an effect completely terrifying; while the sable volumes of smoke now rolled heavily around the demon and his proselyte, with a degree of heat and denseness, which to any thing human, not expressly strengthened and upheld by supernatural aid and interference, would certainly have threatened suffocation. The moon moreover, whose mellow light might otherwise have served to abate the horror of the scene, had indeed risen high in the silvery horizon; but about this period her mild lustre became obscured by clouds heavily laden, which only heightened its tartarean solemnity. With these low gusts of wind (the usual prelude to a shower or tempest) began to arise also, fanning the brightening flames as they swept over the monastery, and augment-

ing

ing their fury, until, growing to a hurri-
cane, their noise again resembled the bel-
lowing of angry bulls, as each succeeding
blast howled over the adjacent hollows,
and among the rugged promontories of the
mountain.*

Amid this deafening uproar, and these
appalling symptoms of impending destruction, the pale abbot Obando, suspended
over the burning wreck of his convent,
seemed holding close communion again
with his demoniacal deliverer; while beneath him the frequent shock of weapons
announced the desperate conflict which
had taken place between the banditti and
the resolute officers of the holiest of tribu-
nals; and around him roared an elemen-
tary confusion, of which the most fanciful
hypochondriac could scarcely form any
accurate conception.

Meanwhile

* The reader must excuse this second introduction of
bull-roaring, as perhaps after all this is only a Spanish
comparison; bull-fighting is a popular amusement in Spain.
I have heard it often, I confess, but cannot vouch for the
accuracy of the similitude.

Meanwhile the scene below was equally turbulent and novel in its nature to the secluded inhabitants of the monastery of Montserrat. Confusedly hurrying up and down the aisles were seen the timid brotherhood, awaiting with terror and expectancy the termination of the contest furiously kept up between their defenders, the holy officials, and the rapacious marauders of the mountain on which their abode was situated. A few had joined the inquisitorial party, and were actively opposing the further progress of the banditti, not so much from their love of such perilous exercise as fighting appeared to them, as from a desire to evince their zeal, in the presence of its servants, to aid the cause of the blessed tribunal, and demonstrate their readiness to arm in its service, in hopes of receiving, should the event prove fortunate, some suitable recompence; while the rest were endeavouring to extinguish the flames, or wandering through the galleries, listening to the unwonted

din

din of discord, in visible consternation and
dismay.

"Lord have mercy upon us!" muttered
the aged Geronimo, who composed one of
the latter number—"saint Mary intercede
for us! here is a goodly affray for holy
and peaceable men like myself to be engaged in! Blessed Virgin, end it quickly,
to the confusion of thine enemies, I pray!"
' "Fold thy robe closer around thee," here
interrupted Jacopo, who happened to be
passing hastily, armed with a burning
splinter, and bleeding in several places—
"fold thy robe closer around thee, brother,
and furnish thee with something, if it be
only a fragment of a stool or platter-stand,
of which thou mayst find plenty in the
refectory, and aid us to repel these Philistines in their bold and bloody outrage!"

"Under favour, brother," replied the
humane Geronimo, startled at this dangerous proposition—"under favour I would
rather to the surgery, since some of you,
I see, have received hurts which may need
mine

mine utmost skill to cure: besides, I remember me at this moment of a vow I
have taken, to be patient and pacific under
whatever circumstances——"

Geronimo wou'd fain have finished his
sentence; but Jacopo was beyond hearing;
so they parted, one to evince his interest
in this desperate brawl, and the other to
prepare his medicines for those whose
mangled bodies might survive its termination.

The deep bell of the monastery had
pealed one over the heads of the combatants, and still the contest continued with
unabated ardour on both sides. The robbers, little expecting a reception of the resolute kind they experienced, were only
rendered more than usually desperate, by
the desperation of their enraged leader,
and the apparent hopelessness of their
cause; while the members of the Holy Tribunal, accustomed to overcome every obstacle, preserved their coolness and forti-
tude even amid the most imminent dan-

ger; for against the assaults of these ruffians, their long close garments of sable
cloth, which covered even their visages,
and gave them rather the appearance of
demons than men, were little or no defence. With regard to the assistance afforded them by the fraternity, it was very
inconsiderable; their total want of defensive weapons, and utter ignorance of the
art of warfare, rendering them rather ridiculous objects of compassion, than an available accession of strength to the party
they espoused.

CHAP.

CHAPTER XXVI.

Then echoed wildly from within,
Of shout and scream the mingled din,
And weapon clash, and maddening cry
Of those who kill, and those who die !

Scott.

WHILE thus the conflict was raging within the holy walls of the monastery, from which a broad column of flame and smoke was now ascending, that nearly reached the elevated haunt of the banditti, Corvetta, and a single one of that devoted band (the rest having descended to reinforce their leader) were standing on a small projecting fragment of their airy habitation, surveying the progress of the devastating flames below. Her companion in this melancholy occupation was the wounded and lately-insensible Gomez, whose head was now enveloped in ban-

L 4   dages,

dages, and who still seemed excessively faint from the loss of blood he had endured, but who watched with angry impatience the proceedings·of his comrades, which he hoped would terminate in the final demolition of the pile he saw blazing beneath him.—" May curses wither the strong hand," he exclaimed, " which rendered me incapable of assisting in this night's glorious enterprise ! felled to the earth by a lazy, drivelling monk—a lubberly, athletic mendicant !—the foul fiend fly away with him !"

" Speak softly, Gomez, when we talk of fiends !" now exclaimed Corvetta, suddenly, who was his sole auditor in that desolate region, " for look—I see a bright form hovering yonder, amid those sulphury wreaths of smoke, which surely bears the shape of nothing earthly !"

" Nor heavenly neither," now muttered Gomez, in evident alarm, while his teeth began to chatter, and his knees to tremble; " and

" and see, a monk in his arms, by all that is horrible!—oh, saint Mary save us!"

" Ha! ha! ha!" rejoined Corvetta, unable to resist the impulse she felt to laugh at him for his cowardice, though its tone resembled more the cry of terror than the sound of merriment—" thou wilt be a monk one day thyself, good Gomez, or Corvetta is a false——but hist! I think I hear voices!"

Corvetta was not deceived, at least in this latter surmise, for now rung feebly every surrounding chasm to the loud deep voice of Obando, who exclaimed, sickened at the dreadful proposals of the demon, and almost suffocated by the sulphureous atmosphere which enveloped him—" Oh that I were again a solitary palmer, pursuing my thorny path barefooted to the shrine of the holy city, for then would there be comfort at the end of my pilgrimage!—oh that I were again the humble malecontent, droning away a despised life among the inhabitants of yonder burning

L 5   fane,

fane, for then would there be hope at the termination of my miseries!"

" This is no answer!" here cried a shriller voice, which Corvetta and her shivering companion rightly judged could only belong to the fiend himself.—" Dost thou repent thee of thy league with Zatanai, reject his services, and prefer destruction?"

" I do repent!" was heard faintly, but fervently, to proceed from the lips of the monastic; and a moment after, the ascent of a clear shower of sparks from the smouldering ruins beneath, proclaimed the fall of something heavy amongst them. The demon was still seen hovering alone for a transient period, as if glutting his infernal appetite for torture with the last writhings of his unhappy victim, and then gradually disappeared.

" God have mercy!" exclaimed Corvetta, joining her hands now earnestly together. " God have mercy—he is gone!"

" Whom meanest thou is departed?" demanded Gomez, who had long since averted ed his gaze in horror from this strange and appalling scene.

" Both! both!" returned Corvetta, unclasping her hands suddenly, and placing them over her forehead, as if to recall in retrospection the hideous sight she had just witnessed, " both! both!"

Gomez hereupon ventured to look up, and beheld the truth of what she asserted. A silent glance of terror and astonishment passed even between these hardened partisans of a no less hardened chief, and they mutually seemed to relinquish the subject. But though Gomez and Corvetta stood long watching the doubtful progress of the strife beneath them, it is extremely dubious whether they at all observed what they appeared to be intently gazing at, so strong was the impression left on them both, by the singular and incredible appearance they had witnessed.

During this period, the renowned sanctuary of Montserrat was the scene of a no less direful tragedy, albeit the principal

events

events therein were of a different description.   The banditti, on their entrance, had
been resolutely encountered by the members of the inquisitorial party, whom the
monks had gladly admitted to their assistance, formed into a compact body, with
the holy standard in the midst of them:
this sable phalanx, however, the rude assaults of the banditti, with their heavy
carbines and keen cutlasses, soon succeeded
in dispersing, or, at least, in putting out
of order.   This once effected, the indivi-
duals of that holy body fought afterwards
at great disadvantage; inasmuch as the
robbers were more accustomed to such
straggling modes of combat, and possessed
greater dexterity of hand and limb than
their opponents.   From that moment,
therefore, while hand to hand the hardy
ruffians battled it fiercely with their anta-
gonists—

        " The wild confusion, and the swarthy glow
     Of flames on high, and torches from below,

                                             The

The shriek of terror, and the mingling yell—
For swords began to clash, and shouts to swell,
Fiung o'er that spot of earth the air of hell!"

and long and desperately did the conflict continue, without the least apparent advantage on either side. At last the robbers began to grow weary of such a succession of sharp blows, at the hands of adversaries from whom it was likely, after all, but little plunder would be obtained; which reflection, very probably, subsequently tended to slacken their exertions.

As is frequently observable in such cases, the courage of their opposers seemed to increase with the momentary panic which appeared to spread itself among the marauders, when another event changed suddenly the prospects of the contending parties. Roldan, who, from the moment of his having gained admission to the monastery, had been diligently employed in searching for Isabel, attended only by a small party of his bravest followers, the rest being committed to the command of the

the lieutenant, now returned disappointed and distracted, not having been able to discover either Isabel or her supposed paramour, Obando, to the aid of his companions. Like an infuriated tiger he rushed among his enemies, and dealt his blows around with an effect almost inconceivable, incessantly endeavouring to animate his associates by his words and his example.

About this period, moreover, arrived the whole remnant of the banditti, whom Corvetta had dispatched to the assistance of their leader—an addition of force which made even the inflexible and wary inflictors of inquisitorial vengeance retreat to the very centre of the chapel, of which they had heretofore defended the entrance against the main body of the pillaging banditti; but which holy sanctuary, aided as they were by Alfieri and Fernandez, commanding a numerous posse of monks and peasantry they found it impossible to preserve from profanation. Here, therefore, stationing themselves, they resolved
to

to " conquer or die" in defence of their
position; and many a desperate struggle
ensued, the result of which was the loss
of many a drop of precious blood to the
determined combatants.   Roldan, as he
prosecuted the work of carnage vigorously
around him, often called loudly on the
name of the absent superior, and defied
him to single combat a second time in
vain.   Obando was nowhere to be found :
then turning to his dauntless followers, he
strove, by encouraging words, to inspirit
them to even additional intrepidity, by
occasionally exclaiming—" Oh ! bravely
done, Sebastian—Pedro, thy single arm is
worth a million of piastres: thou shalt
share gold enough for this to-morrow.
Pikestaves and trenchers, all are come
against us !" he continued, half-ironically,
as he lifted again his ponderous hanger to
smite one who appeared amongst the foremost of his adversaries.

" In the name of our holy church, I
excommunicate that hand for ever!" exclaimed

claimed an insignificant, spare-looking figure, on whose uncovered head the blow
had descended—this was father Jacopo.
The courageous little monk staggered beneath the heavy fall of the hanger, the
edge of which having glanced aside, luckily entered not the scull so deep as might
have been apprehended: he fell, notwithstanding, senseless from the wound, and
fortunately Roldan did not repeat the
stroke.

Transient, however, was the triumph of
the fierce chieftain who had caused his
overthrow; for Alfieri de Gracy and Fernandez, with a choice few of the stoutest
inquisitors, had now succeeded in hem-
ming him round so completely, that he
found it impossible any longer to avoid
the doom which he merited. A blow
from De Gracy, which struck the yellow
feather from his bonnet, and a thrust from
Fernandez, which, although it entered not
his body, was violent enough to throw
him off his guard, became the signal for a
general

general attack on him. He soon fell, overwhelmed with numbers, and wearied out with carnage, while instantly

> " A score of pikes, with each a wound,
>   Bore down, and pinned him to the ground ;"

from which he was never again destined to arise. On witnessing the fall of their leader, and perceiving that Sebastian himself was badly wounded, the banditti began to view their chance of escape as desperate, and suffered no opportunity for flight to pass unheeded: flight however was now not so easily accomplished, the breach through which they had entered being guarded by a troop of officials and peasantry, stationed for the purpose of intercepting them. This was done truly in the unrelenting spirit of the Inquisition, who never permitted a victim in their power to escape from condign punishment, and as victims, it was evident, these hungry bloodhounds now regarded the remainder of this devoted band.

Several

Several of them, nevertheless, on the present occasion, paid dearly for their addiction to extermination and cruelty; for the robbers, finding themselves thus mercilessly devoted to destruction, resolved not to fall easy sacrifices: none submitted, for none expected clemency; a few maimed wretches, whose course was betrayed by the blood which marked their footsteps, effected a retreat, and the rest were eventually hewn in pieces before sunrise.

CHAP.

CHAPTER XXVII.

But see, his face is black, and full of blood !
His eyeballs farther out than when he lived,
Staring full ghastly, like a strangled man !
His hair upreared, his nostrils stretched with struggling :
His hands abroad displayed, as one that grasped
And tugged for life, and was by strength subdued.

                              SHAKESPEARE.

THE tumult had now subsided, and, save
where a few forlorn stragglers of the banditti yet struggled for their lives, the monastery was hushed in comparative tranquillity. A heavy shower of rain from
the overcharged clouds, aided by the exertions of the brotherhood; had partially
extinguished the flames which had enveloped one side of the edifice; and the fraternity of Montserrat appeared in a fair
way of speedily surmounting all their difficulties. Alfieri de Gracy was directing
                                        the

the inexperienced monks in the best method of preserving their convent from the
further ravages of the flames, and aiding
in their total extinction; while Fernandez de Leon had flown on the wings of
love to Isabel, who had been previously
disposed of in a place of safety, near the
foot of the mountain, with permission to
reconduct her to the arms of her father,
whom a slight wound rendered incapable
of much present exertion.

Obando was still missing; and, apart in
one of the chambers of the monastery, a
party of the officials were engaged in taking the depositions of the brotherhood
respecting his extraordinary disappearance.

At this juncture was observed, slowly
pacing the chapel, and often stooping to
discern the plight of such of the unhappy
victims of that fray as wore the monastic
garb, with whose bodies the floor was li-
terally strewn, the venerable form of the
certainly not over valiant, but benevolent
Geronimo. By his side was still standing
the

the meagre figure of Jacopo, for whose wound the good old monk Geronimo had found an appropriate plaister, albeit he still exhibited considerable symptoms of pain and lassitude. They were mutually engaged in the laudable design of rendering the last mournful services to their deceased or dying brethren; for such as had drawn their last earthly breath; they dropped a pious bead, and perchance a silent tear; and to those who yet possessed the power of " fixing their dull gaze" for a few minutes longer, they presented the crucifix, as the symbol of salvation; while often, as they bent over each succeeding prostrate form, the expression of their countenances, and especially of Geronimo's, demonstrated that the deceased had formerly been an intimate acquaintance, or it might be a zealous and confiding friend.

While they were thus busied in performing the last rites of Christianity to the dying sufferers, a loud and slow-drawn effort at suspiration immediately attracted
their

their attention. They turned, and beheld
stretched on the gory pavement, at a little
distance from them, a tall figure in monastic habiliments, which the imperfect
light alone prevented their instantly recognising, and both accordingly advanced
towards it. A convulsed heaving of the
drapery around him, as he lay prone on
his face in the centre of the chapel, was
the only intimation they now received of
the sufferer being still in existence; when
gently raising him betwixt them, the
monks discovered, to their utter consternation and astonishment, the wan com-
plexion and haggard lineaments of the already proscribed abbot—the malecontent,
Obando!

The first impulse of Jacopo was to deliver him immediately up to the Inquisition; but if his companion Geronimo
was more cowardly in the fray, he now
dared to act with more decided courage
and humanity than his associate in the
pious task he had undertaken. With
many

many significant gestures he intimated to
Jacopo his conviction that the unhappy
wretch could not survive many minutes;
together with his own unwillingness to
deliver him to the authority of that dreadful tribunal, or its emissaries for even so
short a space of time, when he was so
soon to answer for his iniquities at the bar
of the Almighty Judge. With these
sentiments Jacopo seemed reluctantly to
acquiesce; while Geronimo continued to
uplift the unresisting object of their terror
and commiseration, who yet seemed con-
scious of their sympathy, although much
too deeply absorbed in horrid and bewil-
dering ruminations to express his gratitude.
—" Unholy brother! art thou here?" was
the first exclamation of Geronimo, as soon
as terror and amazement permitted his
utterance.

" Here!—where?" exclaimed Obando,
rolling his hollow eyes frightfully around
the blood-polluted chapel, on the figured
sides of which the expiring flames yet
flung

flung a red and truly infernal radiance.—
" Oh, true! in the dusky regions of never-
ending wretchedness—the dark and gloomy
realms of interminable misery, where pleasure is never tasted, and repose is unknown—where the malevolent gnash their
teeth in vain, for their torments are eternal!—where my companions are devils
(here Geronimo drew back, and Jacopo
dropped his compassionating hold of the
abbot's garment)—the ravisher, the man-
slayer, and the apostate! No," he continued, as if suddenly recollecting himself
—" no! I have repented—ha! ha!—I
have repented! Off then, fiends! ye have
no power to harm me now—I have repented!"

" Hast thou, poor wretch?" faintly articulated Jacopo, who still seemed half-
inclined to leave the consolation of the
guilty abbot to his scarcely less terrified
companion: " then may our holy Saint
receive thee!"

" What voice is that which utters holy
sounds?"

sounds?" cried Obando, still endeavouring
to raise himself higher, and with his dim,
sunken eyes, searching the meagre visage
of the monk who had spoken—" what
voice is that which utters holy sounds?
He—*he* was holy, righteous, bountiful!—
he, who in this very sanctuary, fell a
thrice-honoured martyr to the cause he
loved—the cause he was engaged in—the
cause of righteousness, whose end is peace!
What cause had I to kill him?   Oh! he
was holy—*he*, the abbot Ambrose! who
remembers him not?—who mourned not
for him?   That did even I who slew him
—that did the malecontent who murdered
him.   I saw the writhing form sink down
helpless at my feet—I seized the gasping
throat—I strained the quivering nerve—
I suffocated him! the red stream gushed
from his pale, writhing lips! it hath gushed ever since—it gushes now: it hath
floated the marble with gore," he wildly
continued, gazing on the ensanguined
pavement of the chapel, which the red

glare still rendered dimly visible—" it hath floated the marble with gore—it hath clogged up my path to heaven—it hath rendered my soul too heavy to mount— it hath rendered my spirit too wretched to supplicate. Still, still it weighs me down—I cannot shake it off me! when I would soar, blood—blood is in my path, and all my efforts are unavailing. I sink —I sink, baffled by a load of crime!— darkness gathers around me—the gloom of hell pervades my downward course, and I strive to ask for clemency in vain! Despair is mine associate—demons have seized me—guilt drags me down, and to eternal perdition will my deeds consign me!" As he finished, he sunk, totally exhausted, into the arms of the horror-stricken Geronimo, whose humanity would not suffer the already-lacerated form, even of the wretched criminal before him, to become a second time dashed on the pavement, while his own aged arms possessed
sufficient

sufficient strength to sustain his weight from further injury.

" Holy Virgin !" now muttered Geronimo, while supporting the weak form of Obando on his bosom, " can this man belong to the blessed?"

" Whom meanest thou?" again demanded Obando, rousing himself hastily from the torpor into which he appeared to have fallen. " I tell thee he is blessed, and thou art not wise to doubt of his felicity. I watched his dying pallet as he lay stretched before the illumined shrine —I saw the light fade from his altered aspect—I viewed ye all shrink from him— *him*, Augustine! ye deemed him accursed, because ye beheld him wretched; but none knew the cause of his wretchedness —none, save Obando! I tell thee, he is blessed, since the malady which afflicted him had not its origin in his own evil heart: his heart!—it was not evil, though it yearned for the iniquities of another. But he kept his oath—he died, and kept

M 2 his

his oath! yet, look! he lives—still lives!
—see where he mounts amid the burning
fragments—amid sparks that scorch him
not, and flames that cannot consume him!
Even such a look he wore on that dire,
fatal night, when discovered in the clois-
ter, holding forbidden intercourse, I bound
him solemnly to secrecy. Now see—he
smiles on me, and with a benignant wafture of his hand, instructs me to look upward for consolation! Blessed shade! I
obey thy silent dictate: airy phantom! I
soon shall follow thee."

As the abbot uttered these incoherent
speeches, Geronimo occasionally looked
fearfully around him; and it is averred,
that he afterwards confessed he saw a form
resembling the deceased father Augustine, but much superior in magnitude,
slowly ascending among the smouldering
ruins of the edifice: but whether the good
monk was deceived, by a wavering column of smoke, a wreath of morning vapour, or otherwise, I shall leave the sagacity

city of the reader to determine; not choos-
ing to take wholly upon myself the re-
sponsibility of answering for that of which
many in this incredulous age might be
apt to question the veracity. On breath-
ing the last syllable of the preceding pas-
sionate burst of declamation, Obando appeared even yet more exhausted than
heretofore; and it now became plain that
his dissolution was at hand. He sunk
again into the arms of him who was yet
willing to support him, and, growing
fainter and fainter, appeared ready to yield
up the ghost. The monks shuddered,
turned up their eyes expressively, and
hung over him in dreadful and inexpressible consternation and expectancy.

Jacopo, after a transient pause, again
displayed the holy cross before him, and,
with mute solicitude, by signs exhorted
him to repentance; while Geronimo endeavoured to open his cumbrous habit, for
the purpose of prolonging his existence for
a few wretched moments, by admitting

the reviving air. But now it was that the cause of his death became visible; on tearing aside his attire, the brothers observed with horror the ghastly injuries his body had sustained in the stupendous fall he had received, on resolving to forego the protection and support of the yellow spirit of the monastery: his joints were broken, or dislocated—the ribs appeared to be fractured—the entrails ready to protrude; in short, the spectacle which Obando now presented was too horrible to be described. Shocked at such an unexpected sight, Geronimo hastily closed the garment, and, making a final effort, gently laid the suffering superior upon the ground, rightly conceiving that posture to be best calculated for affording him ease. The abbot Obando turned his dying visage once more towards him; and fixing his glazed eyes upon his countenance, with an expression of thankfulness which could not be mistaken, he murmured with emotion, while the breath of mortality seemed to to linger unwillingly upon his lips.—" I have little hope in the world to which I am summoned, except——" and the rest of the sentence was too imperfectly pronounced to be comprehended by his auditors.

The brethren looked anxiously upon each other—life seemed hovering, ready to depart, upon the yet quivering lips of Obando.—" He has little hope, except ——" repeated Geronimo, looking steadily in the wrinkled visage of his companion.

" Except our hearts and our voices be employed for his salvation," said Jacopo, suddenly: " then," added he, turning abruptly towards the expiring abbot, " it shall be so: a hundred masses shall be duly said for the repose of thy sinful soul." Jacopo afterwards became abbot of Montserrat's monastery; and he kept his word.

Obando survived just long enough to hear this assurance repeated to him, and then expired. The myrmidons of the Inquisition, by this time returning from the

M 4   slaughter

slaughter of the banditti, rushed to seize their victim; but they received his lifeless body in their arms.

Fernandez de Leon, accompanied by his precious charge, returned before dawn to the convent, where, the flames being totally extinguished, and the devastation they had effected found to be inconsiderable, comparative tranquillity was again restored. The monks received them with joy; and ere they departed from the monastery of Montserrat, he received in due form the hand of his adored Isabel, whose heart he had possessed long before; and there was not long wanting the society of his early-lamented mother (the reported bride of Roldan, Corvetta, who now made no scruple of abandoning his fastness), to render his felicity truly enviable.

It now becoming incumbent on the brotherhood to elect a new superior, Jacopo was by universal assent selected to fill that important station: his avarice was acknowledged; but as it was a fault of which

which they were aware, they contrived to guard against it, and he discharged the duties of his office with equal credit to himself, and profit to the fraternity. Gomez, almost the only survivor of the lawless horde to which he had belonged, fulfilled the prediction of Corvetta, by becoming a monk of the order; while the rest of his former companions paid the forfeit of their iniquities with their lives, several being found, on the morning which succeeded the combat, concealed in glens to which they had escaped, where they had died during the night of their wounds. For Roldan, whose incautious procedure had caused the overthrow of his band, his body being thrown upon the mountain, as unworthy of burial, was devoured by birds of prey and ravenous animals; while, to manure the adjacent wilderness,

" His mouldering bones the winds dispersed,
Unwept, unhonoured, spurned, and curse

Alfieri de Gracy having bestowed his

M 5   blessing

blessing on the union of Isabel with Fernandez de Leon, went shortly afterwards
with them to his estate near Barcelona;
where, under his auspices, and those of
Fernandez, the union of Carlossa with
Inez was speedily effected. This happy
couple, after continuing several years in
the service of their newly-married patrons,
were presented by Alfieri with a small
farm in the vicinity; whither I shall anon
transport the reader, that he may be enabled to form an adequate conception of
their happiness.

Meanwhile Corvetta resided principally,
for the remainder of her life, at the man-
sion of Fernandez; but was never known
to omit visiting once a-year the spot which
had formerly been the haunt of the banditti at Montserrat. With respect to the
sight she had witnessed, together with
Gomez, on the night of the combat (viz.
the suspension of the malecontent in the
air, by infernal agency), having been enjoined by her confessor to secrecy, she
                                    spoke

spoke but little: yet it was evident that scene had left a strange and indelible impression upon her mind, and assisted to work the partial alteration which had taken place in her sentiments.

The body of the late abbot Obando was honourably interred in the cemetery of the monastery; the testimony of Jacopo and Geronimo, in corroboration of his having died a holy and Christian death, as was exemplified by his having requested that prayers might be repeated for his deliverance from purgatory, being believed in preference to the aspersions of his enemies, who, since death had removed the object of their dislike and apprehension, had considerably relaxed in their endeavours to defame him. Yet still, to the inquisitive traveller, will the superannuated tenants of that venerable pile narrate incredible stories of the yellow spirit of the monastery, unconscious perhaps of the after derision they excite, or the emotions of of compassion, occasionally mixed with scorn, which they awaken in his bosom.

———

Twelve years had passed—twelve rolling summers had elapsed, since the events we have narrated, when a solitary pair of travellers, whose habits bespoke them of some monastic order, stopped at a little cottage in one of the most romantic situations Catalonia afforded. It was near the balmy close of an autumnal evening, and the setting sun shed his departing radiance on the most delightful scene imaginable. If any description could do justice to such a combination of beauties as the eye encountered, that of the noble bard in panegyrizing " this delicious land," might be deemed admirable—

" The horrid crags, by toppling convent crowned,
　The cork trees hoar that clothe the shaggy steep,
The mountain moss, by scorching skies imbrowned,
　The sunken glen, whose sunless shrubs must weep,

The

The tender azure of the unruffled deep,
  The orange tints that gild the greenest bough,
The torrents that from cliff to valley leap,
  The vine on high, the willow branch below,
Mixed in one mighty scene, with varied beauty glow."

At the door of the cottage they were met
by its rustic owner, and the smiling partner
of all his toils and pleasures, surrounded by
a group of rosy children, whose prattle was
hushed at the appearance of the reverend
strangers. In the visages of the monks
were discernible the features of Geronimo
and the reformed Gomez, now father Nicholas, and, in the ruddier aspects of the
peasants, those of Carlossa and the faithful Inez. And now, having entered the
cottage, into which they were welcomed
by the liveliest demonstrations of joy, Carlossa knelt before the elder of his revered
guests, and, while Inez was busy in preparing their entertainment, humbly requested his blessing.

"The blessing of saint Mary be upon
thee, my son," said the holy Geronimo,
and a tear trickled down his aged cheek

as

as he spoke—" the blessing of saint Mary be upon thee, and tarry with thee, for thou hast deserved it!"

His companion Nicholas seemed equally affected; but spoke nothing. Carlossa knew not, nor could divine the cause of their emotion; but the profound respect he entertained for the characters of these holy men permitted him not to inquire the origin of that grief which had awakened his sympathy before he knew its object. The repast was by this time spread (for they knew the holy fathers would return that night, and the monastery was at some distance), and the monks partook thereof in silence, which was only once interrupted by Carlossa venturing to inquire after the welfare of Fernandez and Isabel. The reply was, that both wore well, and in the full enjoyment of as large a portion of this temporal world's blessings, as was permitted to fall even to the lot of the virtuous. To them therefore Carlossa rightly judged the evident uneasiness of the

the fathers could not possibly appertain, as it was plain their purpose, at this distance from the convent, was to visit the sick couch of some expiring penitent, whose soul was about to seek its eternal resting-place. After reposing themselves for a transient interval, and partaking moderately of such refreshments as were placed before them, the monks arose.

" A draught of water, and a little bread," said Geronimo, while preparing to depart, " will suffice the wants of life, and I sorrow to have tasted more. Farewell, son! for the present. I am homeward bound; and must not this day be a loiterer: the moon will be up ere the night be spent, and should we be belated, her beams will light us to the monastery. I have yet to tell my rosary a hundred times, for the safe passage into Paradise of another erring soul—he who was called Alfieri de Gracy is no more !"

The mystery was now elucidated. Carlossa sank on his knees in an ecstacy of sorrow

sorrow and of gratitude (for Alfieri had been his principal benefactor), and the travellers departed on their journey.

FINIS.

Printed by J. Darling, Leadenhall-Street, London.

NEW PUBLICATIONS.

[6c

NEW PUBLICATIONS.

	£.	s.	d.
Very Strange, but very True, or the History of an old Man's Young Wife, by Francis Lathom, 2d edit. 4 vols.	1	0	0
The Feuds of Luna and Perollo, a Romantic Tale of the Sixteenth Century, 4 vols.	1	2	0
The Midnight Wanderer, or a Legend of the Houses of Altenberg and Lindendorf, by Margaret Campbell, 4 vols.	1	2	0
Father as he Should be, by Mrs. Hofland, Author of the Clergyman's Widow, &c. 2d edition, 4 vols.	1	4	0
Fatal Revenge, or the House of Montorio, a romance, by the Reverend C. Maturin, 2d edition, 4 vols.	1	4	0
Beatrice, or the Wycherly Family, by Mary White, 4 vols.	1	6	0
The Confederates, by the author of Forman, Wharbroke Legend, &c. 3 vols.	1	1	0
Winter in Washington, or the Seymour Family, 3 vols.	0	16	6
Torrenwald, a romance, by Scriblerus Secundus, 4 vols	1	6	0
Principle, by Miss M'Leod, author of Tales of Ton, &c. 4 vols.	1	2	0
Some Account of Myself, by Charles Earl of Erpingham, 4 vols.	1	0	0
Grandeur and Meanness, or Domestic Persecution, by Mary Charlton, author of Wife and Mistress, Pirate of Naples, Rosella, &c. 3 vols.	1	1	0
Preference, by Selina Davenport, author of Donald Monteith, &c. 2 vols.	0	12	0
St. Clair of the Isles, or the Outlaws of Barra, 3d edit. by Elizabeth Helme, 4 vols.	1	0	0
Oriental Wanderings, or the Fortunes of Felix, an Egyptian Romance, 3 vols	0	18	0
Helena Egerton, or Traits of Female Character, by the author of Always Happy, and Claudine, 2 vols	0	10	0
Frederick Morland, by the author of Lochiel, 2 vols.	0	14	0
The Insurgent Chief, or O'Halloran, an Irish Historical Tale of 1798, 3 vols.	0	18	0
The Robber Chieftain, or Dinas Linn, by Nella Stephens, author of De Mowbray, 4 vols.	1	2	0

[4c

NEW PUBLICATIONS.

[1 c

NEW PUBLICATIONS.

	£	s.	d.
Augustus and Adelina, or the Monk of St. Bernardine, a romance, by Miss C. D. Haynes, 4 vols.	1	0	0
Sisters of St. Gothard, by Elizabeth C. Brown, 2 vols...	0	10	6
St. Margaret's Cave, or the Nun's Story, by Mrs. Helme, new edition, 4 vols.	1	2	0
Soldier of Pennaflor, or a Season in Ireland, 2d edition, 5 vols.	1	10	0
The Advertisement, or Twenty Years Ago, 2d edition, 3 vols.	0	15	0
Iskahder, or the Hero of Epirus, by Arthur Spencer, 3 vols.	0	15	0
The Castle of Villa Flora, a Portuguese Tale, by a British Officer, 3 vols.	0	16	6
The Black Convent, a Tale of Feudal Times, 2 vols ..	0	11	0
Man as he is, by the author of Man as he is not, 3d edition, 4 vols	1	0	0
Castle of Santa Fé, a romance, 2d edition, 4 vols.	1	0	0
The Highlander, a Tale of my Landlady, 2 vols	0	11	0
Bravo of Bohemia, or the Black Forest, 2d edit. 4 vols. ,	1	0	0
Hesitation, or To marry or not to marry, 3 vols... ...	0	18	0
The Intriguing Beauty, and the Beauty without Intrigue, a tale, 3 vols............................	0	18	0
Disorder and Order, by Amelia Beauclerc, author of Montreithe, &c 3 vols.	0	16	6
Dacresfield, or Vicissitudes on Earth, by Cordelia, chief Lady of the Court of Queen Mab, 4 vols.	1	0	0
Leolin Abbey, by Miss Lefanu, 3 vols...	1	1	0
Veteran, or Matrimonial Felicities, 2 vols............	1	1	0
Saragossa, or the Houses of Castello and De Arno, a romance, by E. A. Archer, 4 vols...............	1	4	0
Wild Irish Boy, by Rev. C. Maturin, 2d edition, 4 vols.	1	2	0
Runnemede, an Ancient Legend, by Louisa Sidney Stanhope, author of the Bandit's Bride, &c. 3 vols..	0	18	0
The Outcasts, a Romance from the German, by George Soane, post 8vo. 2 vols.	0	16	0
Past Events, by Mary Charlton, 3 vols................	1	1	0
Priest of Rahery, a Tale, by the late W. Parnell, Esq. M.P.	0	5	6

[2 c

GOTHIC NOVELS

An Arno Press Collection

Series I

Dacre, Charlotte ("Rosa Matilda"). **Confessions of the Nun of St. Omer,** A Tale. 2 vols. 1805. New Introduction by Devendra P. Varma.

Godwin, William. **St. Leon: A Tale of the Sixteenth Century.** 1831. New Foreword by Devendra P. Varma. New Introduction by Juliet Beckett.

Lee, Sophia. **The Recess: Or, A Tale of Other Times.** 3 vols. 1783. New Foreword by J. M. S. Tompkins. New Introduction by Devendra P. Varma.

Lewis, M[atthew] G[regory], trans. **The Bravo of Venice,** A Romance. 1805. New Introduction by Devendra P. Varma.

Prest, Thomas Preskett. **Varney the Vampire.** 3 vols. 1847. New Foreword by Robert Bloch. New Introduction by Devendra P. Varma.

Radcliffe, Ann. **The Castles of Athlin and Dunbayne: A** Highland Story. 1821. New Foreword by Frederick Shroyer.

Radcliffe, Ann. **Gaston De Blondeville.** 2 vols. 1826. New Introduction by Devendra P. Varma.

Radcliffe, Ann. **A Sicilian Romance.** 1821. New Foreword by Howard Mumford Jones. New Introduction by Devendra P. Varma.

Radcliffe, Mary-Anne. **Manfroné:** Or The One-Handed Monk. 2 vols. 1828. New Foreword by Devendra P. Varma. New Introduction by Coral Ann Howells.

Sleath, Eleanor. **The Nocturnal Minstrel.** 1810. New Introduction by Devendra P. Varma.

Series II

Dacre, Charlotte ("Rosa Matilda"). **The Libertine.** 4 vols. 1807. New Foreword by John Garrett. New Introduction by Devendra P. Varma.

Dacre, Charlotte ("Rosa Matilda"). **The Passions.** 4 vols. 1811. New Foreword by Sandra Knight-Roth. New Introduction by Devendra P. Varma.

Dacre, Charlotte ("Rosa Matilda"). **Zofloya;** Or, The Moor: A Romance of the Fifteenth Century. 3 vols. 1806. New Foreword by G. Wilson Knight. New Introduction by Devendra P. Varma.

Ireland, W[illiam] H[enry]. **The Abbess,** A Romance. 4 vols. 1799. New Foreword by Devendra P. Varma. New Introduction by Benjamin Franklin Fisher IV.

[Leland, Thomas]. **Longsword,** Earl of Salisbury: An Historical Romance. 2 vols. 1775. New Foreword by Devendra P. Varma. New Introduction by Robert D. Hume.

[Maturin, Charles Robert]. **The Albigenses:** A Romance. 4 vols. 1824. New Foreword by James Gray. New Introduction by Dale Kramer.

Maturin, Charles Robert ("Dennis Jasper Murphy"). **The Fatal Revenge:** Or, The Family of Montorio. A Romance. 3 vols. 1807. New Foreword by Henry D. Hicks. New Introduction by Maurice Lévy.

[Moore, George]. **Grasville Abbey:** A Romance. 3 vols. 1797. New Foreword by Devendra P. Varma. New Introduction by Robert D. Mayo.

Radcliffe, Ann. **The Romance of the Forest:** Interspersed With Some Pieces of Poetry. 3 vols. 1827. New Foreword by Frederick Garber. New Introduction by Devendra P. Varma.

[Warner, Richard]. **Netley Abbey:** A Gothic Story. 2 vols. 1795. New Introduction by Devendra P. Varma.

Series III

Curties, T. J. Horsley. **The Monk of Udolpho; A Romance.** 4 vols. 1807. New Foreword by Devendra P. Varma. New Introduction by Mary Muriel Tarr.

Green, William Child. **The Abbot of Montserrat; or, The Pool of Blood.** A Romance. 2 vols. 1826. New Introduction by Frederick Shroyer.

[Harley, Mrs. M.] **Priory of St. Bernard**; An Old English Tale. 2 vols. [1789]. New Introduction by William E. Coleman.

Helme, Elizabeth. **St. Margaret's Cave: or, The Nun's Story.** An Ancient Legend. 4 vols. 1801. New Foreword by Frederick Garber. New Introduction by Devendra P. Varma.

[Kelly, Isabella]. **The Abbey of St. Asaph.** A Novel. 3 vols. 1795. New Introduction by Devendra P. Varma.

[Maturin, Charles Robert]. **The Wild Irish Boy.** 3 vols. 1808. New Introduction by E. F. Bleiler.

Meeke, Mrs. [Mary]. **Count St. Blancard, or, The Prejudiced Judge.** A Novel. 3 vols. 1795. New Foreword by Devendra P. Varma. New Introduction by John Garrett.

Roche, Regina Maria. **Nocturnal Visit.** A Tale. 4 vols. 1800. New Foreword by Robert D. Mayo. New Introduction by F. G. Atkinson.

S[helley], P[ercy] B[ysshe]. **Zastrozzi, A Romance and St. Irvyne; or, The Rosicrucian: A Romance.** 2 vols in one. 1810 and 1811. New Foreword by A. J. Hartley. New Introduction by Frederick S. Frank.

Smith, Mrs. [Catherine]. **Barozzi; or The Venetian Sorceress.** A Romance of the Sixteenth Century. 2 vols. 1815. New Introduction by Devendra P. Varma.